SUCKER PLAY

Grady Haskell lay in the dirt outside the Canyon House saloon. His empty holster lay limp at his side. His shirt was ripped where his star had been. His clothes reeked of whiskey poured over him, bile was sour in his throat, and his ears still burned from Rutt Dubison's contemptuous words:

"I can know some respect for a smart man, Deputy, but I hate to give even breathing room to a dumb one. You're not even worth killing—unless you keep hanging around."

First Haskell had been bushwhacked in the dark without a chance to spot his assailants. Now he had been suckered in public into laying down his guard just long enough. Dubison and his crew must still be roaring with laughter. Haskell knew just one thing could drown out that sound.

The click of a gun being cocked—and the blast when the firing pin drove home. . . .

Also by L. P. Holmes
and available from Popular Library—

BRANDON'S EMPIRE
04370-9 $1.75

CATCH AND SADDLE
04400-4 $1.75

HILL
SMOKE

by L. P. Holmes

POPULAR LIBRARY - TORONTO

The characters, places, incidents, and situations in this book are imaginary and have no relation to any person, place, or actual happening.

HILL SMOKE

Published by Popular Library, a unit of CBS Publications, the Consumer Publishing Division of CBS Inc., by arrangement with Dodd, Mead & Company, Inc.

ISBN: 0-445-04435-7

Printed in Canada

10 9 8 7 6 5 4 3 2 1

HILL
SMOKE

1

THEY SAT in Sheriff Bill Hoe's office, waiting the arrival of the night freight. Having chewed one black cheroot to a ragged stub, Bill Hoe tossed the soggy remnants into the battered cuspidor beside his desk and searched a vest pocket for a fresh smoke.

He was a seamed, grizzled man, gone somewhat to flesh about the waist and shoulders. A full quarter century of service behind the star had given him a considerable wisdom concerning men and their ways; a knowledge of their few virtues and their many vices, of their occasional nobility and their too often staining meanness. However, the years had also taught him deep patience and a realistic tolerance. Now, with a new cheroot burning between his teeth, he put his glance on Grady Haskell and slowly spoke.

"This is a hand you'll have to play one card at a time, son. The Trinity Hills hold their share of private feuds, but also there's a clannishness in them that can shut every door in your face. Occasionally, however, some word does manage to leak out, as it did when the whisper came down the trails that Frank Gentile was in that country somewhere.

"Well, hereabouts we want Frank Gentile for the Bella Coola Mine payroll robbery, for the two killings that went with it, and for jail-break. Over in Fredonia County they want him for the Lockeford Bank job and the dead man he left there. So, when the word reached here, I sent Jack Breedon into the Trinities to see if he could come up with Gentile.

"Which suited Breedon fine, for he was on duty when Gentile broke jail, and so felt more or less responsible. That was six months ago, and there's been no word from or of Jack Breedon since. It's as if he'd ridden off the edge of the world. I don't want the same to happen to you."

Grady Haskell shifted a lean, hard body in his chair, gone restless with waiting.

"We won't worry about that."

Erect, he would have stood an even six feet, with a wiry, all-over physical competence definitely apparent. His features were blunt, weathered to a deep brownness. Against this his eyes were a clear, cold shade of gray—eyes slightly puckered as though behind them a questioning speculation was constantly at work.

"You say," he went on, "that Gentile broke jail. What kind of a breakout was it?"

"Through the roof. At midnight check the prisoner was in his bunk, apparently asleep. In the morning he was gone. It was a case of nobody's fault and everybody's fault. The jail was old. No one had ever dug a hole through the roof before, so we presumed nobody ever would. You know how such things are."

"You think Gentile had outside help?"

"Possible, though I doubt it. Certainly there was no sign of it. And he ran pretty much alone."

"And since this deputy of yours, this Jack Breedon went into the Trinities, there's been no word of him or from him. Would you have any idea—why?"

Bill Hoe shrugged, shook a grizzled head.

"Nothing that wouldn't be a long guess. Like he might have located Gentile, with things going to a shootout, and Gentile getting there first."

"In which case you'd think some word of such would have come through, wouldn't it?" argued Haskell.

Bill Hoe shrugged again. "Not necessarily. The star has never been too popular in the hills. And that damn country is full of secrets. Which is why I want you to slip in there as quiet and casual as possible."

"You call it a hand to be played one card at a time," Haskell said. "Does that mean I'm free to make my own rules as I go along?"

"It does," Bill Hoe assured. "I'd ask no man to take on such an assignment and then tie his hands with a lot of do and don't restrictions. All I ask of you is a measure of decent judgment, which I know you'll show. Else Arch Wilcoxen would never have recommended you. I will say this. By all means we want Gentile, if you can come up with him. But mainly your chore is to find out what's happened to Jack Breedon."

Through the slow minutes of another half hour they discussed the various angles of the problem. Then, as a short pause of silence fell, a faint, far off cry came winging in across the night; the wailing, lonely bay of a train whistle breaking through Spanish Gap, five miles east of town. Bill Hoe stood up and reached for his hat.

"That's our freight, son."

They left the office, stepping into the dark run of Ordeville's main street. It was a clear night, with the stars all one vast, scattered glitter. At this hour—eleven o'clock—the street was empty, the town asleep. When Grady Haskell remarked on this, Bill Hoe nodded his satisfaction.

"Suits our purpose fine. The less folks around to see, the less to wonder and talk. The less talk, the less chance of word traveling."

9

The railroad station, with its freight yard and cattle pens, was south of town beyond an interval of some hundred and fifty yards. As Grady Haskell and Bill Hoe crossed this, a light went on in the station house. Bill Hoe chuckled drily.

"About now, Blaney Daggett is cussing mad. He's a lazy old bear and hates having to get up this time of night. If he had his way, no trains would run except between sunup and sundown. Your horse ready, son?"

"Ready and waiting."

They moved past the corner of the station house and stood beside the tracks. Across the flat run of the earth the train's headlight was an on-rushing, gargantuan eye, boring a cone of radiance through the night.

The station door opened and Blaney Daggett emerged, carrying a lantern. True to Bill Hoe's prophecy, he was mumbling mild profanity. Bill Hoe jibed him gently.

"Now, now—Blaney! If it wasn't for the night freight you never would see the stars. And to look at them occasionally is good for a man's soul."

"My soul gets along better on sound sleep," growled Blaney peevishly. "Your man ready? Corbin will be yelling his head off because he had to stop at Lockeford for that extra empty."

"He'll get over it," Bill Hoe soothed.

At the near end of the cattle pen a horse stamped and nickered plaintively. Grady Haskell went to the animal, quieting it with murmured words and the sweep of a hand along its neck.

Now the rails set up a metallic humming, which grew swiftly in pitch and intensity as the freight came storming on. Again the whistle wailed, flinging a long banner of sound against the night sky. Then the bell began a measured clanging.

The engine crunched by, hissing and rumbling, firebox shedding a flickering, crimson glare. Brake shoes chattered as they gripped, gave, then gripped again, while draw-bar and coupling set up an on-running, but diminishing clatter. With a final creaking jolt the train made its complete stop.

Lanterns swung down from the caboose and came hurrying. One was carried by Corbin, the freight conductor. Impatient words snapped out ahead of him.

"All right, Daggett—all right! I've got your damned empty for you and there's a loading chute in it. So get done—get done!"

Brakemen ran out the loading chute and Grady Haskell led his horse up the cleated steepness of this into the echoing emptiness of the box car.

"That's it, Corbin," Bill Hoe told the freight conductor. "Now all you have to do is haul him to Rancheria Creek, unload him there and then forget the whole business."

Mollified by the briefness of the halt, Corbin mellowed somewhat.

"Fair enough," he said gruffly.

Bill Hoe stuck his head in the door of the car and called through its blackness.

"Good luck, son!"

Hours later, in the cold gloom of early morning, the train pulled away from the Rancheria Creek crossing, leaving Grady Haskell there to climb into his saddle and point his horse's head to the north. Riding thus, he watched the late stars pale and fade, and as dawn broke grayly across the world, he saw the Trinity Hills shouldering up in front of him.

These heights were deep timber country, climbing through slope and bench and ridge to far, misty distance. Haskell closed in on them across the lifting swell of juniper dotted foothills and made stop on a little flat where Rancheria Creek emerged from the first timber edge. Here he off-saddled, letting his horse roll and drink, after which, from the frugal pack behind his saddle he produced a feed of oats for the horse and a small, fire-blackened pot in which to brew up some coffee for himself.

He spent a full hour crouched over his meager fire, savoring the black, hot goodness of his coffee, smoking brown paper cigarettes and soaking up the fire's fading warmth as the flames shortened to ruby coals, then to gray ash.

With day's first sunlight filtering across the hill slopes, he saddled again and moved into the timber, striking a faint trail which followed beside the quickening waters of the creek as it wound along a gulch which climbed between steepening walls.

In time these walls gave back, and the trail led into a long meadow which spread its full half mile of green lushness through an ever widening corridor of drowsing timber. At the far end of this, cattle grazed.

Here the creek waters ran leisurely, glinting in the rays of a climbing sun which distilled a resinous fragrance from the ranks of pine and fir. Haskell filled his lungs deeply and decided that these Trinity Hills were good country.

He was half way along the meadow when sudden, rushing movement erupted from a creek-side willow thicket out ahead. A pair of timber wolves, shaggy, tawny-gray, dodged into the open, pursued by a wild-eyed cow, whose gaunt, foam-flecked flanks were heaving and shaking from sustained effort. In the depths of the thicket a calf bleated feebly.

Engrossed in their deadly intent, the wolves, for the moment, were unaware of Haskell's presence. Lunging wildly back and forth, the cow swung hooves and horns at the killers. They eluded her with darting ease, their snarling, chopping fangs a constant taunt and threat.

12

The distance was a good eighty yards, much too far for any kind of certainty with a belt gun. But there was a rifle riding in the scabbard under Haskell's knee and he lifted this free, levered a cartridge into the chamber and drew quick bead on the nearest wolf.

Perhaps instinct, or the flicker of outside movement, broke through the slavering killer's savage absorption. It flung up a startled, prick-eared head, and for the space of a long breath was motionless. Haskell's rifle whipped out its hard, flat report and the bullet slammed home, knocking the wolf flat.

The brute rolled over and over, snapping at the spot on its side where the bullet had struck. Then it was up on its forelegs, dragging into the willows. Fast as a beam of light, the other raider was beyond the thicket and gone before Haskell could lever home a fresh cartridge.

The cow, with legs spread and head low, a hoarse bellow deep-rumbling in her throat, came ponderously around, ready to face any new threat. As he rode up, Haskell grinned at this show of bovine truculence.

"All right, you gallant old idiot. Behave yourself!"

Reassured at sight of a man and his horse, the cow, though watching carefully, kept her distance and her peace as Haskell dropped his rifle into the scabbard and dismounted.

Drawing his belt gun he pushed into the willow thicket. Off to one side there sounded a choked but rising snarl and the chop of fangs, and there was struggling movement as the wounded wolf reared a savage head. Haskell drove a quick shot into that narrow, venomous skull, then worked his way to where the calf lay, new-born, its soft baby eyes bulging with terror.

Looking it over, Haskell saw it was uninjured, and knew relief as he reholstered his gun. He had feared

13

finding a fang-torn little animal to be put out of its misery.

"Poor scared little devil," he muttered. "We'll get you out to safer ground."

He carried the calf into the open and balanced it across his saddle, swinging up behind it and sending his horse on along the meadow. Rumbling an occasional bellow of anxious, plaintive concern, the mother cow followed close behind.

As he neared the scatter of grazing cattle, further movement at the timber edge off to his right, caught and held Haskell's glance. Three riders showed there and came on swiftly. Reining up, Haskell swung his horse to face them, his casual, musing ease of the moment replaced by an impassive alertness.

Two of the three were men, the third a girl. One man was an oldster, gaunt and still-faced. The other, younger, loomed burly in the saddle. Under sun-bleached brows his eyes were hot and intolerant, his broad face high colored with the strong flush of arrogance. He threw rough demand at Haskell.

"Just where the hell do you think you're going with that calf?"

Haskell regarded him steadily. "Who's asking?"

"Tendler is the name. Once more—where with the calf?"

"Right about here should do."

Speaking, Haskell stepped down, lifted the calf free and watched it wobble off on uncertain legs, to be immediately reclaimed by its anxious mother.

"Smooth," Tendler jeered. "Caught with the goods, you would just put it down and ride away. Is that it?"

Once more astride, Haskell faced this arrogant fellow with a quickening anger.

"Mister, you talk like a fool!"

Tendler rocked forward in his saddle, as though

14

struck a physical blow and about to retaliate. Whatever his intentions, the girl headed them off with quick words.

"Easy, Vince! I'll handle this." She measured Haskell with intensely blue, wary, and frankly hostile eyes. "I am Katherine Levening. Hayfork is the Levening brand, and that is a Hayfork cow and calf. As I can not recall ever seeing you before, I'm wondering what possible legitimate interest you could have in Levening cattle?"

Here, Haskell saw, was strong pride and its usual accompanying mood of wilful authority. She sat her horse with a natural ease and held his glance steadily. She wore clothes that were plain and workaday; a divided skirt of faded khaki, a tan wool blouse, and a short jacket of buckskin, gone shiny and stained from long use. Lone concession to adornment was a silk scarf at her throat, of a color to match her eyes. Her head was bare and her hair, drawn back in a roll at the nape of her neck, glinted blue-black in the sunlight.

"It's simple enough," Haskell explained. "A pair of wolves were after the calf. The cow was trying to hold them off. I shot one wolf, the other got away. I thought it a good idea to move the calf closer to the rest of the cattle in case the second wolf came back for another try."

"Now that's pretty smooth, too," charged Tendler. "It sounds all right, but I've got to be shown."

Haskell twisted and pointed. "That willow thicket back yonder is where you'll find the dead wolf. And," he added bluntly, "if such isn't proof enough to suit you, you can make anything you damn please of the rest!"

Arrogance remained in Vince Tendler, and hot intolerance still fumed in his pale eyes. But these were things now tempering under a deepening caution. Hands folded across his saddle horn, he leaned forward and studied Haskell narrowly, recognizing the fact that here was no casual drifter to be threatened and bullied and easily cowed.

"All right," he conceded, "we'll see if there's a wolf. Go have a look, Sandy."

The older rider nodded, reined away at a lope. Haskell thumbed tobacco and papers from a pocket, spun up and lit a cigarette. Through the pale drift of smoke he again put a steady glance on Katherine Levening.

She was turned slightly, watching Sandy. But that she was fully aware of Haskell's interest, showed in the deepening color washing up her throat and through her cheeks. In profile she lost none of her attractiveness. This girl possessed a clean, striking beauty. When she began to stir uncomfortably under his regard, Haskell switched his direct attention to Tendler.

"You should have heard my shots—two of them."

"We heard no shots," Tendler denied.

Still watching Sandy, the girl said, "Which doesn't prove that there were none, Vince. Sound doesn't travel very far in the timber."

"Well now," murmured Haskell dryly, "that saves me being classed the complete liar. Obliged."

Down meadow, Sandy pulled to a stop beside the willow thicket. He studied it for a moment from the vantage of his saddle before dismounting and pushing into it. Shortly he reappeared, swung up and came jogging back.

"Wolf in there, all right," he reported. "Fresh killed. Shot twice. As big a lobo as I ever saw."

Taking a final drag of his cigarette, Haskell stubbed the butt on his saddle horn and looked around.

"Everybody satisfied?"

"Not entirely," Tendler said. "We could be wondering where you came from and where you're heading?"

Haskell shrugged. "My business and none of yours. And now, if the lady is satisfied that my intentions with a Hayfork cow and calf were strictly honorable, I'll be on my way."

There was an unintentional bite to his words which sent color again washing through the girl's cheeks. Briefly, a combative spark blazed in her eyes. But it was a challenge which faltered and fell away, and she made no reply.

Surprisingly, gaunt old Sandy took care of this. He fixed Haskell with a level stare and spoke gruffly.

"Far as I'm concerned, you gave us the whole truth about the cow and calf. But Mister, I don't like the way you said what you just did. Mebbe you better beg Katie's pardon!"

"Never mind, Sandy," the girl said quickly, her voice subdued. "We—I—probably deserved that."

"No!" growled the old fellow sturdily. "You don't ever deserve short talk from anybody. Well, Mister?"

Meeting Sandy's uncompromising stare, a glint of humor crinkled Haskell's eyes.

"Old timer," he said, "you're all right. If there was more to my words than necessary, I gladly beg the lady's pardon."

So speaking, he gave Katherine Levening a final direct glance, touched his hat, then reined his horse across the meadow and into the timber. He rode with apparent unconcern until safely from sight, when he left his horse and prowled back afoot until he had clear view of the meadow again.

They were still as they had been, grouped in discussion. Presently reaching agreement, they split up. Katherine Levening and Vince Tendler heading out of the meadow along the creek trail, deeper into the hills.

Sandy, putting his horse to a fast walk, fixed his glance on the meadow sod and followed the hoof sign Haskell's mount had left.

Retreating to his saddle, Haskell went his way again. From time to time, where timber and terrain made it possible, he checked on Sandy and found the gaunt rider sticking doggedly to his trail.

Grady Haskell had never been in these Trinity Hills before. To all reasonable intents and purposes, the incident of the wolves and the Hayfork cow and calf had been satisfactorily explained and accepted. Yet, here was persistent interest being shown in him.

Riding out the miles and hours, he soberly pondered this fact.

2

THE ROAD CAME narrowly in from the timber, spanned the river by means of a log bridge and so entered the flat. Half way across this it spread to several times its normal width for a little distance, then returned to size again as it left the flat and lost itself once more among the pines. This wider stretch, lined on either side with a ragged run of buildings, comprised the meager limits of the town of Reservation.

On three sides the timber pressed solidly in, as if grudging the town occupancy in these hills. On the fourth, the north side, gaped the mouth of the dark and craggy rift which spawned the river waters and, to a very considerable degree, dominated the town.

It lacked an hour of sundown when Grady Haskell rode into Reservation. He came slowly, the tired hoofs of his blaze-faced dun striking up a muffled echo on the log bridge. Immediate concern being shelter for the dun, he rode the full length of the street before locating the feed stable and stage corral at the far end. Passing through, he made a guarded survey of the town and found this interest returned in full.

At a saloon hitch rail several saddle mounts stood slackhipped, while beneath the overhang of the building their riders lounged. Idle talk among these men ceased and they watched in heavy silence as Haskell passed. One of them inclined his head and pulled his hat lower, as if to shield his eyes from the rays of the westering sun, now slanting in under the overhang. The maneuver seemed casual enough, but it also served to shelter his face from full view. There was a furtive caution in the move which Haskell did not miss.

Beyond the saloon a spring wagon and team were drawn up in front of a general store. Two men were loading some supplies into the back of the rig. One was a lank, bleached man in worn ranch clothes, the other, stocky and round of face, was wearing a store-keeper's canvas apron, well dusted with the whiteness of flour. Engaged in some sort of amiable discussion, they too became still and eyed Haskell carefully as he went by.

Further along, past several lesser buildings on the south side of the street, a hotel lifted its weather-beaten, two storied height. All across the front of this ran a galleried porch on which a matronly, middle-aged woman had just finished a chore of sweeping. She stepped to the edge of the porch, leaned on her broom and watched Haskell all the way to the stable.

Here, at the far end of a narrow, shadowy runway a roustabout appeared and came along almost silently over the litter of straw and chaff underfoot. He was shiftless and dirty and rancid with an accumulation of stable odors, and there was a guarded uneasiness in his small, faded eyes as he watched Haskell rein in and step from his saddle. When he spoke, his words were as surly as his manner.

"What'll it be?"

Here, thought Haskell, it was again. The same wary suspicion and poorly veiled hostility he'd felt all along the street, and, for that matter, all through these Trinity Hills. It was, he decided, about time to meet the attitude head on.

"What in hell do you think? What's a man usually

want when he rides into a stable late in the day on a weary and hungry horse?"

Haskell's stare was as bleak and demanding as his words, and the roustabout had no luck in answering either. His glance slid away and he reached for the dun's rein.

"Charge is two-bits a night for general holding in the corral. For a stall, a manger of timothy and a feed of grain half a dollar."

Haskell gave him a dollar.

"See that the stall is clean and well-bedded, and the manger of hay and feed of oats extra generous. Finally, there'll be a good currying and brushing down."

With saddlebags over his shoulder and rifle under his arm, Haskell went out into the street and angled back to the hotel. He crossed the porch of this into a lobby that was plain and square and frugally furnished. Off to the left a door led into a small parlor, while on the right an archway opened into a dining room now echoing pleasantly with the rattle of dishes as tables were being set for the evening meal.

At the inner wall of the lobby, tucked against the foot of a flight of stairs leading to the upper floor, was the register counter. Leaning against this, chewing on a cold cigar, a heavy man with a blocky face and a roach of iron-gray hair, eyed Haskell with a glance much too disinterested to be convincing.

Haskell lowered his saddlebags to the floor and stacked his rifle against the counter. He spun the register and signed his name boldly.

The man with the cigar studied the signature a moment, then put his glance on Haskell again.

"No address?"

"No address."

"Me," said the man with the cigar, "I'm Amos Potter. I own this place. When a man stays with me I like

21

to know where he comes from as well as what his name is."

"The name," Haskell said, "is my own. If you must have more, put down any place you want. But it won't mean anything." He gathered up his gear and fixed Amos Potter with steady eyes. "Well—yes or no?"

Potter considered, chewing at his cigar. He shrugged and handed over a key.

"Number Two. Corner front at the head of the stairs. We eat at seven, twelve and six."

The room had a single window which looked out on the street and across town to the canyon mouth and the climbing run of misty hill country beyond. An iron bed, neatly made up with clean blankets, stood on a square of worn, but well-swept carpet. There was a wash stand with heavy, white china pitcher and basin, and beside a wall bracket lamp a small mirror hung. Finally, there was a round-backed chair with its legs firmly braced with a criss-cross of twisted wire.

Haskell dumped his saddlebags on the bed, stood his rifle in a corner, deciding that he'd known far worse lodging. He stripped to the waist, his shoulders and chest startlingly white against the deep-burned brownness of his face and neck.

He sloshed water into the china bowl and had himself a good wash. Toweled dry, he donned his shirt again and combed his dampened hair with his fingers. He pulled the chair up to the window and slouched far down, wholly relaxed against the fatigue of a past sleepless night and long day in the saddle.

In sluicing away the dust and grime of travel, it seemed he had in part also washed away some of a shell of hard, taciturn remoteness, and as he carefully fashioned and lighted a brown paper cigarette, he became a younger, easier man. He sent a thin line of

22

pale blue smoke from pursed lips and mused back over the events of the past three days.

Seventy-two hours ago he'd been in Iron Mountain, listening to Arch Wilcoxon explain that his old friend, Sheriff Bill Hoe, at Ordeville down in Bovard County, wanted to borrow a deputy for a spell, a smart man and level headed, who could also be more than passably tough when the occasion required. Also, who had never been in the Trinity Hills country before. And Wilcoxon had decided that he, Grady Haskell was the one man who fitted these qualifications perfectly.

So here he was in this little mountain town of Reservation, faced with another law chore which could, he reflected ruefully, turn out to be as mean as any he'd ever tackled. For plainly, these hills were renegade country, sanctuary for men on the dodge; the wanted ones, the hunted ones, no doubt many with a price on their heads. For such, the measure of continued freedom, even life itself, meant constant wariness and suspicion and a distrust of all other men.

Seeking information among this sort, as word from one man about another, would be not only difficult, but also more than casually dangerous. There could be so easily a shot from the dark or a knife in the back. . . .

The original idea had been that he drift into the Trinities like any other rider on the dodge. This, so Bill Hoe had reasoned, would allay any suspicion of his real purpose. But matters hadn't worked out that way at all, decided Haskell. So far, all he'd met up with had been suspicion and hostility. Knowing a stir of returning grimness, he concluded he'd ride along with Bill Hoe's theory for a time, but if it continued to show no better results than it had so far, then the gloves would come off and he'd go at things his own way.

Hoofs beat a hollow echo on the log bridge and he straightened his chair and looked out to see riders leaving town. The spring wagon still stood in front of the store and now beside it were three men. The third of these was Amos Potter, the hotel owner.

Haskell watched these three, noting their gestures and the evident vehemence behind their talk. Sardonic pressure thinned his lips. He, a stranger, had ridden into town, and now all was a stirring and an uneasiness. Very definitely, Bill Hoe's theory of anonymity wasn't working out worth a damn.

The three broke up. The rancher climbed into his wagon, gathered up the reins and kicked off the brake. He made some final remark, emphasizing it by the sweep of his hand, which the storekeeper answered in kind. Then the rig made a dust scattering turn in the middle of the street and rolled out of town.

Frowning with speculative thought, Haskell lay back in his chair again. Presently he shrugged, closed his eyes and fell into a doze.

The jangle of a supper gong spreading its mellow resonance through the hotel and along the street, roused him from his brief nap. He got to his feet, yawning and stretching, and paused for another look out the window.

Full sundown held the town, all its parts being drowned in blue shadow. Over north, the mouth of the canyon was a cold looking cauldron of smoky mists. Reflected sunset glow, fast fading, touched timber tips on some lofty ridge points. Stirring air seeped in at the open window, bringing with it a faint chill and a vigorous essence which was the twilight breath of this country.

Drifting up from below, coffee fragrance reached

24

him, and immediately hunger was a raw, insistent need. He left his room and dropped down to the lobby, which was astir with activity. Several men were passing through on their way to the dining room. And, standing by the register counter, was Katherine Levening. She gave him a grave and guarded scrutiny, but made no sign of having seen him before.

She had, he thought, lost none of her clean, cool beauty. As before, she was bareheaded, and her hair had a windblown look, as though she'd been riding fast. Quelling an impulse to nod to her, Haskell held her glance steadily.

Here he recognized the same high, wilful pride, but with it now was the shadow of uneasiness. As he passed her eyes fell away and she turned, putting her back to him.

The long central table in the dining room being already well filled, Haskell took one of the smaller ones along the wall. For a time he was content to wait quietly, but as the minutes went by and neither food or attention came his way, irritation and impatience began to stir.

Waiting on table was a girl of some sixteen or seventeen, and the woman who had been sweeping the hotel porch when Haskell rode into town. Both continued to ignore him until the manner of it became too pointed to be other than deliberate design. Finally, when the girl happened to pass fairly close to him, he lifted a hand.

"I'm here," he drawled. "Alive and hungry. Or doesn't that matter?"

She was a sturdy youngster, somewhat sulky looking about the mouth, yet pretty enough in a dusky cheeked, carelessly rebellious sort of way. When Haskell spoke she hesitated, looking at him with dark, uncertain eyes.

Swiftly the older woman interfered.

"You tend the main table, Ruby," she ordered. Then, to Haskell with some severity before moving away again. "You'll just have to wait your turn."

He tried to figure it. It didn't, he reflected, make sense. Owning the hotel, Amos Potter had accepted him as a lodger, advising him also on the times food would be served. Now that food was being deliberately withheld. And for what purpose—unless—

The thought was like a flash of light, and as it registered and took hold, he was swiftly on his feet and out of the room.

The lobby was empty. He crossed this and went up the stairs with quick, soft steps. Outside, early dark was settling in. Here, at the head of the stairs, gloom was thick.

On leaving his room he had closed but not locked the door. It was still closed, but from under it there now seeped a thin glow of yellow lamplight. Listening intently, he picked up the rustle of movement beyond. He twisted the knob, pushed the door wide and stepped through.

Katherine Levening was bending over the bed. She had opened his saddlebags and starting to go through them. Now, with a little gasp of alarm and dismay, she whirled to face him.

"Well, well," he drawled. "This is a surprise. For both of us!"

She was held with a complete stillness, like a startled frightened child might be, not knowing whether to cower or run. Then the high pride began to burn and her head came up and her shoulders stiffened. She met the level severity of his glance with a sort of blind defiance.

"Maybe," said Haskell, not ungently, "there's a reasonable explanation? Though I can't imagine what it

26

would be. Certainly there's nothing in my saddlebags with the Levening brand on it."

She made no answer.

He tried again. "You wouldn't claim it as a mistake, would you? Or that you just happened to stumble in here by accident?"

She finally spoke, with a cold brevity. "I've nothing to say." She moved toward the door.

Haskell stepped in front of her. "It's not that simple, I'm afraid. You've some explaining to do, Katie Levening. Suppose you get at it!"

Instead, she made a darting rush, trying to dodge past him. He stopped her with a sweep of his arm, bringing her around and close to him.

"And you," he murmured sardonically, "were quite ready this morning to make me out a cow thief."

She fought his strength with a slim, desperate fury.

"Let—me—go!"

His grip tightened. "Not so fast! I told you it wasn't that simple. Just what were you up to, going through my gear?"

At first she would not answer, straining to pull away from him. Presently, realizing this as useless effort, she quieted and spoke falteringly.

"I—it really was a mistake. I—I thought—"

"No!" Haskell shook a reproving head. "That won't do. When you walked into this room and lit the lamp yonder to have light to rummage my belongings, you knew exactly what you were doing."

Abruptly she was struggling and fighting again. She got an arm free and beat furiously at him with a small, frantic fist. One blow hammered his lips and he felt the warmth of blood start across them. Quick, ruthless anger leaped in him. He corraled the wild fist and held her helpless.

Her upturned face was close, her eyes wide and al-

27

most black with fear and feeling. A pulse fluttered in her throat and she panted like some captured wild thing. Haskell's words ran harsh.

"So you want it rough, eh? Very well. Seeing that you put blood on my lips, I'll put it on yours!"

He bent his head and kissed her.

She twisted and fought frantically, finally got her mouth free, then flayed him with husky, broken words.

"That—that was an evil, cowardly thing to do. To—to treat me like I was some common—common—! Oh—let me go!"

What she said, and how, for some strange reason cut surprisingly deep. And the little, choked sob which followed, whipped Haskell completely. He dropped his arms.

"Call it what you want. It's also a damn shady business for you to prowl a man's room and rifle his belongings. Doing that, you hardly deserve to be treated like a fine lady. All right, clear out! I guess we're even."

She backed away, scrubbing at her lips, furious with another outburst of seething indignance.

"I—I could have you killed for that! If I just had a gun I'd—I'd—!"

Going down to supper, Haskell had left his belt gun hanging on a bed post. He indicated the holstered weapon.

"Help yourself."

She made no move toward the gun, just scorched him with a final blazing glance, then whirled out the door and was gone.

For some little time Haskell stood quietly, conscious of his leaping pulse. There had been a wild, heady sweetness on Katherine's Levening's lips that carried an impact he hadn't figured on, and which

28

held him now in a long and thoughtful pause. Presently he shrugged, crossed to the mirror by the wall bracket lamp, and there surveyed the damage to his bruised lip. The injury was of small account, and the lingering crimson stain he dabbed away with a moistened towel.

He turned to the bed and the partially disturbed saddlebags. These he emptied, then repacked, frowning slightly as he checked the contents against memory. So far as he could tell, nothing was missing. He had not really expected that anything would be.

For such a person as Katherine Levening was no petty thief. Whatever her purpose in going through his gear, actual theft was no part of it. Yet, what could she have been searching for, unless some means to more fully identify him and his real purpose in these Trinity Hills?

If that be so, why was it so?

The answer to that, he concluded, was something he'd have to wait for.

He put out the lamp and left the room, this time locking the door behind him. Back in the dining room the older waitress stopped beside his table.

"Yes," he remarked casually, "it's all right to serve me now. My room's been prowled. Which was why you wouldn't serve me before, wasn't it? So I'd be delayed until the prowling was done?"

She did not answer, but her obvious confusion told Haskell he was squarely on the truth.

She brought his meal. It was good food and he was very hungry. He enjoyed every bite.

3

UNDER THE STARS the town of Reservation lay physically still, but the throb and rush of white water beating its way through the canyon's high gorge, came down across the night in a solid, sustained rumble of sound. Here and there lamplight pushed out from street windows, but most doors were closed against the thin chill that leaked out of the hill passes with the closing in of full dark. Brightest spots of illumination were the hotel lobby, the general store still open for business, and the town's main bar and card room, the Canyon House.

Moving along the street, Grady Haskell turned in here. Four men were present. One of them, thin and ragged and whiskey punished, was at the far end of the bar, gulping down some stale free-lunch leftovers. Two others were engrossed in a cribbage game at a card table. Leaning on the back of a chair, spectator to this contest, was the bartender. Now, even as Haskell entered, this worthy looked over at the ragged one at the bar and put heavy words on him.

"All right, Peele—you've had enough. I've told you before that one short whiskey don't entitle you to a full meal. If I have to tell you again I'll run you out of this place, once and for good."

The ragged one turned reluctantly away. "Sure, Art," he mumbled. "Sure."

Finally acknowledging Haskell's presence, the bartender straightened, turned and stared. Then, as though begrudging each step, he moved slowly around behind the bar and reached for a bottle and glass. Haskell shook his head, laid down a dollar.

"Some cigars."

He selected a couple of these, trimmed one and set it alight while considering the atmosphere of the place with a mounting distaste. Here was no slightest hint of friendliness or welcome. The bartender had spoken no word to him, just stared with a glance that was stolid and blank and unrevealing. Now, after fanning some change on the bar, he turned his back to fuss at some inconsequential chore. In this lay the final gesture of a surly indifference that set an edge of anger loose in Haskell.

"If I got it, I didn't know it," he said curtly. "For I feel all right."

The bartender looked over the point of his shoulder, spurred at last to speech.

"If you got—what?"

"Smallpox, yellow fever, hydrophobia. You name it."

The bartender stared again. "I don't know what you're talking about."

"The hell you don't! What kind of a place is this? Do you treat everybody like they had the plague? Just how old were you, anyhow—when your disposition soured?"

The bartender flushed, squaring around. He was a paunchy one, with a heavy, veined face.

"You don't like it here, you don't have to stay. And my disposition suits me."

"Then," Haskell told him, bluntly sarcastic, "you're damned easy satisfied."

He dipped his head toward the ragged, thin unfortunate at the far end of the bar.

"Pour him a double shot and take it out of that change. Which should also entitle him to more food. Right?"

The bartender had pouched eyes, surfaced with a watery hardness. He tried to hold Haskell's level, demanding glance, but couldn't make it. He shrugged and reached for the bottle.

"It's your money."

Out in the street again, Haskell went along until the dusty timbers of the bridge were under foot. Here, as if pausing for breath after its headlong, rushing descent from the canyon's heights, the river drifted more slowly. Leaning on the bridge rail, Haskell watched the stars reflect on these quieter waters.

He was no way satisfied over letting his feelings get away from him back there in the Canyon House. He'd had a chip on his shoulder, and for no good reason. After all, it was the bartender's business if he wanted to be surly. It was also his business if he wanted to throw a whiskey bum out of his place of business. Finally, he had finished the cigars asked for. Past that he owed a customer nothing.

Haskell swung his shoulders. In him was an edge of restlessness which hadn't been there when he first rode into this town. What reason for it now?

The episode in his room, perhaps? Katherine Levening, slim and tiger-furious in his arms? Kissing her, he admitted ruefully, smacked of being a fool's move, even if it had been a thing of pure impulse. For impulse, as against coldly ordered thought, had killed more than one man!

Out of the black line of timber came the running mutter of approaching hoofs. Haskell listened for a moment, then left the bridge and dropped back into the sheltering depths of night's deep shadow.

The riders, a dark scatter of them, swept swiftly by,

heads and shoulders bobbing against the stars, hoofs of their horses beating out a hollow thunder roll across the bridge. Behind them, hanging in the chill heavy air, they left the acrid scent of stirred up dust and the broader, more pungent odor of warm, sweating horseflesh. Also, lingered the deep growl of one man's voice and the short, high laugh of another.

They made a massed, hoof-trampling stop in front of the Canyon House, and light beams flashed and broke as the saloon door swung and swung again when men began pushing through. A shadow moved away from the others, angling across street toward the hotel, and a voice called.

"You'll be wantin' a chair in the stud game, Vince?"

"Sure," came the answer. "Hold one for me. I won't be long."

Watching, Grady Haskell lost the man in the street's center darkness, then picked him up again as he crossed the hotel porch through the outflung glow of the lobby windows. When he opened the hotel door and stood momentarily in clear outline against the light beyond, Haskell recognized the arrogant set of the head and the cast of the heavy shoulders. This man, Haskell knew, he'd seen before, earlier in the day. Vince Tendler.

Now, past Tendler's blocky outline a slim figure moved into view. There was no mistaking this one, either. Katherine Levening. She came swiftly up to Tendler and began speaking to him. Then Tendler closed the door and the darkness seemed deeper than ever.

For a long fifteen minutes Haskell stayed as he was, smoking out his cigar. After which he moved slowly back up town. Passing the Canyon House he heard the murmur of men's voices and the sharper, more carrying note of their laughter. He left these sounds

34

behind and came even with the store, where lights still burned, and he recalled a need and turned in here.

Still wearing his flour dusted apron, the storekeeper leaned on his counter under a hanging lamp's down-pouring cone of yellow radiance, making some entries in a ledger. He straightened and faced Haskell with a shrewd, measuring interest.

"Evening, friend," he said.

"Why now," Haskell exclaimed, "that has a welcome sound! The first fair word I've had since riding into this town. And it earns you a sale. Durham. A caddy of it."

The storekeeper reached the tobacco down from a shelf.

"I condemn no man until I know he deserves it."

"You should have a hand at converting some of the others," Haskell observed dryly. "Most act as though suspecting me of horse stealing, or worse."

"We've our share of such, in these hills," the storekeeper said. "Too many of them, as a matter of fact. So it is only natural that the town be a bit wary."

Haskell's cigar had burned to a cold, distasteful stub and he looked about for a place to discard it. Finding none handier, he went to the door and tossed the butt out into the night. Out there in the street's clotted darkness lifted the muted clink of dust dulled spur chains. The sound trailed on by and the door of the Canyon House swung, and it was again the figure of Vince Tendler showing briefly against the light.

Returning to the counter, Haskell spoke carefully.

"You say you've some bad ones in these hills. What's wrong—doesn't the law reach this far?"

"Law headquarters is at Ordeville, a long way off across a big country," the storekeeper said. "And these Trinity Hills are high and deep and wild. As sheriffs go, I suppose Bill Hoe is a good one, for people keep on reelecting him, term after term. And a man can only do so much, he can't be everywhere at once."

Now there were spurs jingling on the store porch and a rider strode in, boot heels chunking solidly. He was a hard-faced one, and he gave Haskell an intent moment of marked interest before turning to the storekeeper.

"Any mail for Hayfork, Jellick?"

"For Hayfork? Hell, no—of course not! Vince Tendler got it yesterday, which you damn well know. And next stage in ain't until tomorrow."

"Now, now, Milo—don't get your roach up," the rider soothed. "No harm in askin', was there?"

So saying, he gave Grady Haskell another quick visual going over, then clanked on out.

The storekeeper, Milo Jellick, stared after him, frowning.

"Now why would Stack Coulter lie like that? He knows Vince Tendler got the mail yesterday. He was with Tendler and waited with the horses while Tendler came in."

Haskell shrugged cynically. "Most likely an excuse to get a close look at me. Though why he'd want to, I wouldn't know. You'd think I had horns and cloven hoofs and a spiked tail. Yes, sir—that I was the devil himself."

Milo Jellick laid a sober regard on him.

"I do not see you as such. But I am wondering enough to ask a direct question. Are you looking for work, or just drifting?"

"Some might call it drifting, some having a look at the country," fenced Haskell. "As for a job, that could depend."

"On what?"

"On where, for who, and for how much. I don't need a job. I got a fair stake in my jeans."

36

Milo Jellick considered a moment, then nodded.

"Just as well. Riding jobs are scarce, hereabouts. The crews are pretty well settled with the two big outfits. That's Hayfork up past the canyon brakes, and Rutt Dubison's Sawbuck layout back on the Beaverhead. The rest of the ranches are one or two man spreads, and they never do any hiring except for an occasional spell of seasonal work."

On the wall behind the counter an ancient, brass-faced clock began a ponderous whirring, then beat out nine measured, mellow strokes. Milo Jellick took off his canvas apron.

"That's it," he said. "Closing time. Makes a long day of it, eight in the morning until nine at night. Drop in tomorrow if you're still around."

Haskell nodded briefly. "Maybe."

He gathered up his caddy of tobacco and moved out to the store porch. Behind him the door scraped to a final closing and the lock clicked. Shortly after, the light went out and now he stood in a thoroughly dark world. He paused there for a little time, to again take measure of this town, and judge the pulse beat of its life.

Here was a town of surly suspicions and guarded words, clinging to the fringe of hill country and dependent upon it for meager existence. A mean little town, thrown together without plan, and void of any semblance of beauty. Out of it, and the hill wilderness round about, he must dredge up two answers. What about Jack Breedon, and what about Frank Gentile? One a man of the law; one a man far outside it. Were these entirely separate problems, or would he find them, as Bill Hoe had suggested might be possible, bound together by some ominous chain of events?

He stirred restlessly. Whatever the problems, they would have to wait until tomorrow. For now weariness closed in on him and thought of bed and blankets was most welcome. A gust of frigid air swept down from the canyon mouth, to drench the town with its damp chill. Haskell hunched his shoulders against the impact, dropped off the store porch and headed for the hotel.

He was halfway across the street before awareness of men around him, came to him. Then it was as though he'd walked into a circle of ambushed wolves. They closed in on him from all sides, fast and wicked.

A shadowy figure rose before him and a driving fist glanced searingly along his jaw. Another blow caught him high on the side of the head, knocking him off balance and staggering. Somebody crashed into him from behind and clubbed him across the back of the neck, close up against the base of his skull.

This was the truly vicious blow, filling the dark with soaring, explosive lights and dropping him to his knees. In this fact was brief fortune for him, as his attackers met in a tangled mass above him, awkward and thwarted by their very eagerness to get at him. Which brief respite gave him time to rid his mind of the first stunned bewilderment and make room for reasoned understanding.

Yet, even as he began to get his thoughts straightened out, one of the group, blocked off from using his fists by the scrambling press, swung a slashing kick. It caught Haskell on the point of the hip and left a darting stab of pain. It did more. It filled Grady Haskell with a blind, wild, destroying rage, and it brought him upright.

He smashed a bunched knee into a man's groin and the fellow doubled up and fell backward, yelling his agony. He found a throat with one reaching, clawing hand and dug savage fingers into it deeply, while using his free hand as a clenched club to beat at the

38

face above. He felt the cartilage of his victim's nose crumple under the fury of his blows, and knew the wish that it might be the fellow's skull.

For a brief moment they gave back, stung by the savagery of his resistence. Then a voice growled thickly:

"Get at him—get at him! Knock the bastard down!"

They came storming back to the attack.

It ran out into a nightmare of man's viciousness toward man. There was no mercy either way, just a snarling, slashing, animal cruelty. There was no sort of ordered thought. There was no count of blows taken or delivered. There was only man's most primitive instinct left, which drove him to fight on and on in blind desperation.

Several times Haskell found himself down in the dust of the street, and several times he came back to his feet again, though not exactly knowing what had put him down or brought him up again. Of only two things was he conscious. No matter how many times he beat off an assailant, there was always another to take that one's place. Then there was the strange numbness now at work all through him.

It had really started with that first blow from behind, the savage smash to the base of his skull. From there, under the cumulative effect of other blows and kicks, it had spread and deepened until now, though dulling somewhat the pain of bruised and punished flesh, it also was stealing away his strength, and making him slow and clumsy and unsure of movement.

He wasn't seeing well either, and getting a weird, unearthly impression of the dark. No longer was it just the night world devoid of light. Now it had become a pool of thick, wooly, black nothingness, in which, it seemed, a man could very well drown. And into this pool he felt himself remorselessly slipping, until he was presently struggling just as desperately to prevent that result, as he was against the physical attack still beating at him.

It was a doomed and losing fight. Both the numbness and the blackness deepened until shortly, despite his best efforts, he lay prone in the dust and knew nothing more.

They milled about his motionless figure. One leaned over him, boot drawn back for another kick. Before it could be delivered, harsh warning came in from the outer dark.

"Leave him be—all of you! Get away from him! You hear me—get away from him! Else I turn loose these loads of buckshot!"

Startled, they scattered and gave back. Someone made heavy, panting demand.

"Who's talkin'?"

"I am—Joe Peele. And before you start laughin', think of this. I'm stone sober, and lookin' at you over the old sawed-off Greener gun I packed when I rode stage express. Now get away from that man!"

Thwarted anger flared back. "You turn that gun loose, Peele—and you'll be dead before morning!"

"I turn this gun loose, you'll be dead before that. Move along—all of you!"

Someone said: "Might as well. No point in workin' over this bucko any more; he ain't feelin' nothin'. He's out cold."

"Yeah," taunted Joe Peele, his words raw with sarcasm. "Out cold. After being gang jumped by all you brave boys." Joe Peele pursed his lips and spat. "Yeah—real brave! Like the times you've kicked me around when I was too drunk to help myself. Well, I ain't drunk now, and there's nothin' I'd more enjoy

doin' than pull both triggers of this gun. I ain't tellin'
you again. Clear out!"

Here was something they didn't care to gamble
with, buckshot lashing at them through the night. So
they drifted off, licking their wounds. Presently sounded the mutter of departing hoofs, and then the deeper
rumble as they crossed the bridge.

It seemed to Grady Haskell that he was crawling up
a tunnel of darkness and silence. Then sound began to
reach him; sound which was at first a meaningless
jumble, but resolved presently into words he could
sort into sense. A force pushing and pulling at him became a pair of hands trying to boost him to a sitting
position. A long, shuddering breath ran in and out of
him and once more he was back in a world of reality.

The owner of the urging hands was saying: "Come
up, friend—come up! Give it a good try now and we'll
have you back on your feet."

He responded with the try and then he was erect,
steadied by his benefactor. He tried to speak, but
found his mouth thick, charged with a salty phlegm
and with clotted blood from his battered lips. He spat,
cleared his throat painfully, spat again. Words came
finally, blurted, ragged and hoarse.

"Where—where'd they—go?"

"Pulled out," was the answer. "You can forget
about them now, friend."

"Forget!" Haskell's voice rode to a harsh croak.
"Like hell! I'll remember—and locate every damn one
of them. Then we'll see how it goes—man to man!"

"Sure, sure. But all that will keep. Right now you
need some looking after."

"You're—who?" demanded Haskell.

"Joe Peele. You bought me a drink in the Canyon
House a little while ago. Remember?"

"Yeah, I remember. Who were—they?"

41

"Hayfork. Vince Tendler and the outfit. I don't know why they jumped you, but I know why they quit."

"You—stopped them?"

"Managed to," Joe Peele admitted briefly. "Now let's get along to my shanty, where you can rest and clean up."

Haskell shook a savagely punishing head with slow care.

"Thanks. But I got a room—in the hotel. I'll be all right. I'm obliged, Joe Peele. I'll see you tomorrow—and buy you another drink."

He pulled away and angled for the hotel.

Never would he have believed the mere act of walking could be so difficult, let alone to move in a reasonably straight line. For the street had somehow become strangely uneven, full of swoops and rolls. Nor would his feet track as they should. His thighs felt thick and heavy, with everything below them numb and unresponsive. Joe Peele called after him anxiously.

"I'd help you to your room if Amos Potter would let me put foot in his damned hotel. But he won't. Now if you'd come along to my shanty—!"

"Tomorrow," Haskell mumbled over his shoulder. "Tomorrow, Joe Peele. I'll see you—then."

He reached the hotel steps, stumbled against them and fell to his hands and knees, the jolt of landing seeming about to split his throbbing head wide open. For a little time he stayed so, eyes squeezed tight against the pain. Then he climbed doggedly back to his feet and went on to the hotel door.

He was fumbling at the latch of this, when it was opened by someone on the inside.

Katherine Levening stood before him. Evidently about to leave for the night, she was buttoned to the ears in a fleece-lined coat, and was carrying a pair of buckskin gloves.

He edged into the full light of the lobby and stood weaving from side to side, looking at her out of bruised, swollen eyes. He tried what he imagined was a mirthless, sardonic smile, but which became instead a bruise-blackened, blood and dust smeared grimace. When he spoke, his words fell thick and uncertain. For now the full effect of a secondary reaction to the beating was setting in. He blinked, pushing an unsteady hand across his face.

"They didn't quite—make it good, Katie Levening. No, they didn't quite—kill me. But they tried, by God—they sure tried! Which makes you out a pretty rough girl, Katie. Next time you want a man killed—order it done, clean. Not beat to death. Girl like you should never hate a man—that bad. Even if he did kiss you. Thought better of you than that, Katie. Really did. Had you figured—different. My mistake, Katie—my mistake!"

Again he passed a hand across his face, as though trying to brush something away. Then he shuffled unsteadily across the lobby.

Eyes wide, her face first flushing, then draining white, Katherine Levening watched this bloodstained, wickedly beaten man reel and weave as he worked a slow, painful way up the stairs. And as the full meaning behind his words struck home, she ran to the foot of the stairs and sent her protest crying up after him.

"I never did! What you say is not true. I set no one after you. I tell you—I never did!"

He paid her no further attention, oblivious now to everything but the necessity of reaching the top of the stairs. He managed it finally and wheeled against the door of his room, leaning there and resting. He knew a sluggish gust of anger over the door being locked, just as he had left it, for now he had to dig through his pockets for the damned key. This he found presently, and after a period of fumbling, got the door open.

Perhaps it was something akin to the instinct of a hurt animal seeking solitude which caused him to lock the door behind him. At any rate he did it, then moved on through the blackness until his legs struck the edge of the bed. With a long sigh he fell forward into the welcome softness of the blankets and let all thought and physical effort slide away.

4

HOURS LATER he wasn't sure whether he'd been hanging on the fringe of unconsciousness, or whether he'd been in and out of a restless, fitful sleep. Once he dimly remembered someone knocking at the door and calling, wanting to know if he was all right. To which he'd given some kind of assurance. Now, fully awake, he knew a demanding thirst.

He slid off the bed and straightened with slow care, flexing muscles and joints gingerly, thankful that the wicked pounding in his head had subsided to nothing worse than a dull ache. Also, he was reasonably solid on his feet once more.

By match flare he located the bracket lamp on the wall and set this alight. After which he lifted the water pitcher from the wash stand and drank directly from it, and deeply. He poured water in the basin and laved his face carefully. First contact was stinging, then vastly comforting. Toweling dry, he examined himself in the mirror.

Physical effects, he decided, were not going to be too bad, though what with various bruises and his cut mouth, visual marks of the affair would be with him for several days. Mental scars—and here a bleak spark shone briefly in his eyes—were something else again. These he would carry until he was able to check them off, one by one, against the men who had put them there.

He limped over to the window and looked out at a world deeply cold and dark. He shivered, turned back and got out of his clothes. He killed the light and crawled into the blankets. Almost immediately he was in a sound sleep.

He awoke to the jangle of the breakfast gong, which also pointed up his hunger. But damned if he was going to hurry! Starting today, this town would have to fit some of its ways to his desires, not the other way around. Bill Hoe had called this a hand to be played one card at a time. But he had also said that he, Grady Haskell, was free to shape the rules to fit the occasion, when such was called for. Which time, he now decided with some grimness, was at hand. The part Bill Hoe had set for him, that of a casual saddle drifter, had brought nothing but suspicion, hostility and a very thorough physical beating. From now on he was going to be exactly what he was, a man behind a star, and tough as toughness was needed!

The breakfast triangle shook another mellow summons through the morning silence. Haskell pushed the blankets aside. He was board-stiff all over. However, by the time he was dressed, bringing a clean shirt from his saddlebags, he had loosened up considerably. His head, while sore to the touch in several places, no longer ached, though still a little heavy. But even this effect was pretty well washed away under the icy tingle of another dousing.

From a deep corner of his saddlebags he came up with a ball-pointed star. This he polished on his shirt sleeve before pinning it in place. He took his gun belt from the bed post, buckled it on, settling it to its accustomed fit. Half drawing the heavy Colt gun, he hefted the comfort of its reality. Last night he'd been caught without it, something, he vowed, that wouldn't happen again.

46

Still limping slightly, he went down to the lobby. Amos Potter was behind the register counter, on which lay a hat. Potter indicated it.

"Yours, maybe? It was found in the street."

It had been brushed clean of dust and cuffed into shape. Haskell nodded as he took it.

"Mine. Obliged. If you're still interested in an address for your register, you can make it Ordeville, or Iron Mountain. Both fit."

Potter was eyeing the star. "That doesn't surprise me too much," he murmured.

"The address?" Haskell queried.

"Or the star," Potter said.

There were few at breakfast, but every eye was on Grady Haskell as he entered the dining room and took a wall table. They looked at a lean, quiet man who moved with some stiffness, and whose blunt, square features were smudged with bruises. They marked the gun at his hip and the badge of authority on his shirt, but when they met his glance they gave way before the cool, steady light in it.

Haskell could find nothing to complain of at this meal. Hardly had he taken his chair than the waitress of last evening was beside him, a fact he remarked on dryly.

"Service I see, has improved." Then, observing the uncomfortable flush that swept her face, he added with some gentleness, "It wasn't your fault. You were probably under orders."

She flushed again, but now the warmth of a quick kindliness showed in her eyes, and as she put his breakfast before him, she murmured low, quick words.

"It was a cowardly thing they did to you last night. That—that Vince Tendler! But you can be certain of this. Katherine Levening did not order it."

With which flat statement she hurried off.

47

Soon, Haskell had the room to himself. Others, starting ahead of him, finished their breakfasts and went about their various business. Lingering over a second cup of coffee, he searched his pockets for something to smoke, but without success. His lips twisted wryly. On leaving Milo Jellick's store last evening he'd had a cigar in his pocket and a caddy of Durham tobacco under his arm. Now he had nothing.

All thanks to the attack. For which, even though it had been Hayfork riders who ganged him, the waitress had assured him Katherine Levening was in no way to blame. Why the emphasis on that fact—if, of course, it was a fact? He was pondering on this when Amos Potter's voice sounded beside him.

"Have one of mine?"

Haskell looked up. The hotel owner, savoring a cigar himself, was holding out a slim Virginia cheroot.

Potter took a chair across from Haskell, leaned back and watched soberly while Haskell got the cheroot alight. Then he made a thoughtful remark.

"No, neither the address or the fact of the star surprises me too much. But I am wondering how long you'll be with us, and why?"

Haskell chose his reply carefully. "Until I get some answers."

"What kind of answers?"

Haskell eyed him levelly. "Pushing on the rope a little, aren't you?"

Potter lifted an apologetic hand. "Didn't mean it quite the way it sounded. Maybe I wanted to help."

"And maybe you'll have a chance to, later." Haskell drained the last of his coffee, shoved back his chair and stood up. He took the cheroot from his lips, looked at it and nodded. "Your taste in tobacco is first class."

Potter came to his feet.

"A minute, Haskell. A point for you to remember. We got some good people in the Trinities, some damn good people! I suggest you don't go jumping at conclusions or forming any hard and fast judgments."

Haskell's glance took on impact. "Just what in hell are you driving at, Potter?"

Potter shrugged. "I said what I wanted to say."

Haskell studied him for another moment in silence, then nodded.

"Fair enough. Once more—thanks for the smoke —and the hat."

He limped out to the edge of the hotel porch. Morning's sunlight was slanting in along the street, as yet its warmth more illusory than real. For the chill that had flooded down out of the canyon during the night, still clung mistily in the hard-angled shadows. The near corner of Jellick's store porch caught the sunlight as strongly as any spot, and here a ragged figure crouched. Haskell stepped into the street and crossed over.

Joe Peele straightened up and crookedly grinned.

"You're made of tough stuff, friend. What you took last night would have put most men in bed for a week."

"Been times I felt friskier," Haskell admitted. "More and more I'm realizing how much I owe you."

"You don't owe me a thing," asserted Joe Peele stoutly. "Last night in the Canyon House you treated me like I was a human being. That makes us even." He indicated Haskell's star. "Maybe, if you'd been wearing that, they'd have left you alone."

"Maybe they would, maybe not. Did I hear you right that it was Hayfork that ganged me?"

"You heard right. Vince Tendler and some of the Hayfork crew. Tendler ramrods for Hayfork. Chesty as hell about it. Way he acts, you'd think he owned the outfit. Mebbe he figgers to some day, if he can talk Katie Levening into marrying him."

Regarding Joe Peele narrowly, Haskell recognized the pinched haggardness, the feverishness which told its own story.

"Yeah," he nodded, "I sure owe you plenty. Had your morning drink yet?"

A dull, shamed flush burned through Joe Peele's liquor punished face. "Do I show it that bad?"

"Come on," said Haskell. "Let's go see if that hombre in the Canyon House has sweetened up any."

He took Joe Peele by the elbow and steered him into the saloon. The owner, Art Oren, was stacking chairs on card tables, preparing to sweep out last night's litter. In a surly silence he circled behind the bar.

"A couple of whiskies for my friend here," Haskell ordered briskly.

Joe Peele's hands shook so badly he could hardly get the first drink to his lips. But with that one down, he steadied, and took the second more leisurely. He glanced toward the free lunch counter, with its stale leavings.

Haskell shook his head. "Hell with that stuff, Joe. A man needs real food to start the day. You come along with me. I know a nice lady over at the hotel. She waits on table, so she must have run of the kitchen."

Joe Peele hung back. "No use. Amos Potter won't let Jennie Wall feed me."

"We'll see about that," Haskell said. "Come on."

He led the way to the rear of the hotel and stepped through the kitchen door. The middle-aged waitress was busy over a pan of dishes. She came around, wiping her hands on her apron.

"Well?"

50

"I've a friend outside," Haskell explained. "He needs a solid meal. I'll pay for it."

"Who is he?"

"Joe Peele."

She sniffed and started to turn away.

Haskell spoke quickly. "I bragged to Joe that you were a nice lady, Ma'am. You wouldn't make me out a liar, would you?"

She paused and came slowly back, meeting his eyes and gravely smiling.

"You've a clever tongue in your head, young man. Very well, I'll feed him. It won't be the first time Jennie Wall has fed a bum."

Haskell reached for his pocket, but she shook her head.

"There are plenty of left-overs. Tell that worthless Joe Peele to wait."

"Not worthless, Ma'am," differed Haskell. "As I rate them, Joe's a pretty good man."

"He's a bum and the town drunk," was the crisp retort. "But I'll feed him."

"Ma'am," said Haskell, "I knew I couldn't be wrong when I told Joe you were a nice lady."

She colored and laughed in small confusion. "Away with your blarney! Tell Joe Peele I'll have his food ready for him in ten minutes. But he'll eat on the steps; I'll not have him in my kitchen. And I expect him to be washed up and looking reasonably christian-like."

Haskell relayed this word to Joe Peele, waved aside his thanks, then circled to the street once more, crossed and climbed the steps of Milo Jellick's store. Jellick, having opened not long before, had come to the edge of the porch to feel the morning sunshine, and now laid his shrewd glance on Haskell.

"So-o!" he murmured. "I was guessing right all the time."

"You mean—this?" Haskell touched his star.

Jellick nodded. "The law has a way of marking men, depending which side of it they choose to ride on. I knew by the set of your shoulders and the look in your eye that you were on the right side."

"I seem to have fooled nobody," Haskell said dryly.

"I am, however," admitted Jellick, "a trifle amazed to see you up and around so early and so lively. For I gathered that last night was somewhat rough."

"Rough enough." Haskell's face hardened at the memory. "You see any of it?"

Jellick shook his head. "Time I got there it was all over and you were in your room. I called at your door, later, to see how you were making out. By your reply you seemed to be doing all right. So I left it that way."

"Decent of you to bother at all," Haskell said gruffly, knowing a growing liking for this rotund little storekeeper.

"Wasn't my idea," admitted Jellick. "Katie Levening asked me to check up on you."

"The devil you say! Why, I wonder?"

"Wondered some on that myself," Jellick said. "Wondered too, why Vince Tendler and his crowd should have ganged you?"

Haskell shrugged. "Your guess is as good as the next."

"I've heard it said," Jellick analyzed slowly, "that some believe a wicked physical beating can put the fear of God in a man, and cause him to leave the country."

"An idea that might work with some," Haskell agreed. "But not here! Would Tendler have cause to fear the law?"

"I have heard of no charge against him." Jellick's reply was a little indirect. "He is not an easy one to judge, is Vince Tendler, for there is a great deal of arrogance and intolerance and quick temper in the man. Now if you had affronted him in some way——?"

"Maybe," said Haskell briefly, recalling the cow and calf and wolf incident of yesterday morning. "We had a word or two back and forth. But with hardly enough in them to set him after me." He was silent for a thoughtful moment before adding: "There might be another reason. But it's a long guess, so I'll keep it to myself." He switched to another subject. "When I left here last night I had a caddy of Durham. Somewhere between here and my room I didn't have it any more. So, I'll need another."

The storekeeper smiled. "I rescued that tobacco myself. Stumbled across it out in the street."

They went inside and Jellick handed the caddy down from a shelf. It was battered and smudged with street dust, but still intact. Haskell broke it open and pocketed two of the tightly packed muslin sacks. Nodding his thanks, he fixed his glance on Jellick with a sudden, blunt intentness.

"Friend, I see you as an honest man who believes in the law. Right?"

"I hope I'm all of that," Jellick said slowly. "Why?"

"You can help me."

"How?"

"With some straight answers to some straight questions?"

"You mean, turn informer?"

"Some might call it so. Sure to if they're on the wrong side of the fence. But decent folk would say it was an honest man aiding what he believes in——the law!"

53

"There could be times when the law is in the wrong."

"Not in this case. Well?"

Milo Jellick considered soberly. "As I said last night, we've undesirables in these hills—perhaps too many of them. I have no use for such and would like to see them cleaned out. On the other hand, we've also some mighty fine people, and I'd never knowingly have a hand in harming any of them."

Haskell made an impatient gesture. "Now there is something I do not understand. Not an hour ago, Amos Potter was making the same kind of talk about the wrong ones and the right ones. Why all the emphasis on that? It gives a man the feeling you're driving at something you're afraid to put into plain language, that you're dodging something. Is that so?"

Milo Jellick's shrug partly closed a door.

"I will listen to you. If I think an answer is justified, I will give it. If I don't—! He shrugged again. "You are interested in some particular person?"

"In two of them. You ever hear of a Frank Gentile?"

"I have. He rode for Rutt Dubison. Whether he still does, I wouldn't know. What do you want him for?"

"Robbery and murder!"

"Why then," said Milo Jellick simply, "I hope you get him. Which may be difficult, even if he is still with Dubison. For, as it is well known by everyone, there are a number of bad ones in the Sawbuck outfit. For that matter, Rutt Dubison is hardly a gentle character himself. I'm not saying he has a record, understand, though he may have. But he is rough—plenty!"

"Interesting," Haskell said, his bruise smudged eyes taking on a speculative narrowing. "Yeah, interesting. Something worth looking into. Now, how about a deputy named Jack Breedon? You ever hear of him?"

54

He was watching Milo Jellick with the finest of attention, and he saw that partly closed door shut fully. The storekeeper bustled around from behind his counter.

"I've my day's sweeping to do and I'd best get at it."

"Friend," charged Haskell, "you're side-stepping."

Jellick faced him sturdily. "If I am, it is my choice. We will leave it so."

"But Jack Breedon carried the star," Haskell reminded with some heat. "You can't write a man like that off as you would some stray coyote."

Milo Jellick turned away. "I have said all that I am going to say."

He picked up a broom, went to the far end of the room and set to work vigorously. The hint was plain.

Baffled, reluctant, Haskell left the store. Here was something to really ponder over. Inquiry concerning Frank Gentile had been answered readily enough— even voluntarily elaborated on. Yet the same inquiry about Jack Breedon had bluntly closed a door in his face.

Frank Gentile was a wanted man, a renegade and a killer. Still, he was just another outlaw, headed inevitably for a violent end, either at the hands of the law, or at those of another of his own kind. To a degree he counted—but only relatively.

On the other hand, disappearance of Deputy Jack Breedon was something that must and would be followed through to a solution, and no amount of evasion could head off that purpose. Certainly Milo Jellick was intelligent enough to understand the distinction and the certainty. Yet he had flatly refused to give answer about Breedon, obviously covering up.

What to do about it?

Nothing more here, Haskell decided ruefully, except ask questions in other quarters and hope to turn up some bit of fertile soil. And if he could raise no results in town, then he'd go to the hills for them. Which meant taking to the saddle again. With the thought he found himself eager for that very thing.

He crossed to the hotel, climbed to his room. Someone had been in here since he'd last left it, for the bed was neatly made up, the pitcher on the wash stand fresh filled with water, the wash basin emptied and rinsed, his saddlebags stacked on the chair.

He left the caddy of tobacco with these, got his rifle from the room corner and went out. In the hall he came face to face with the dusky cheeked girl who had helped wait on table last evening. She had a folded blanket over one arm and a broom under the other. Sight of Haskell plainly startled her and her quick, indrawn breath smoothed the lines of sulkiness from about her lips and left her just what she was, a shy, half-scared youngster.

Remembering from last night, Haskell smiled.

"You're Ruby?"

She nodded, eyes downcast.

"Thanks for making my bed and tidying up my room."

She gave him a swift, upward glance through slanting lashes.

"Why—why—that's all right. Missis Wall, she just can't abide thought of a bed standing all day unmade. I mind what she tells me."

"Mrs. Wall," Haskell said, "is a mighty fine lady. You keep on minding what she tells you, Ruby." He started to turn away, paused. "Ruby—what?"

Immediately the sulky look was about the soft young mouth again. "Just—Ruby," was the sullen reply. She turned and went down the hall, shoulders squared and straight in an instinctive defiance.

Defiance of what? Glancing after her, Haskell wondered. Here, apparently, was another off-center personal angle. These damned hills it seemed, were full of such. . . .

He dropped back down stairs, thankful to find he could now do so without limping and wincing at every step. He left the hotel and saw Joe Peele moving slowly down street. At the same moments hoofs drummed across the river bridge and a single rider turned into town, traveling at a reaching jog, which immediately became a hard-spurred, charging run as the rider sighted the shuffling figure of Joe Peele.

It was a sudden, explosive thing, this change from a casual traveling pace to one of driving purpose. It looked to Grady Haskell like an open attempt to deliberately ride Joe Peele down. Evidently Joe figured the same, and he wheeled frantically for the sanctuary of Milo Jellick's store.

The rider was too fast for him, blocking his way with a rearing, spinning horse. Again Joe tried to dodge, but the rider, with a reaching grab, caught him by the collar of his rusty old coat. He hauled hard on this, trapping Joe's arms, pulling them back and up. Then he again dug in the spurs, launching his horse into a pounding run, upsetting his victim violently and dragging him along, twisting and struggling helplessly, legs and feet furrowing up the dust.

Cold anger was an instant, storming thing in Haskell. He swung the lever of his rifle, chambering a cartridge. Then he was out in the street, rifle at his shoulder. Over the sights he saw the on-racing horse with the leaning figure of its rider who now, half laughing, half jeering, was looking back and down at the man he was dragging. Haskell knew the savage impulse to center on this fellow's chest and loose a shot. Instead, before pulling the trigger, he elevated the muzzle far enough to miss.

The hard smash of report, virtually in its face, made the horse rear and swerve. Also, it caused its startled rider to let go his grip on Joe Peele, who went rolling over and over in a wild sprawl. Again Haskell swung the lever of his rifle, laid it dead in line past the tossing head of the horse, and backed up its authority with harsh command.

"Get off that horse!"

The rider marked the rifle and the bitter chill in the eyes behind the sights. He marked also the star on the shirt of the man holding the rifle. He ran the tip of his tongue slowly across his lips, his expression turning wooden.

Then, very carefully, he stepped from his saddle.

5

THIS FELLOW, Grady Haskell had seen before. Here was the hard-faced one who had come into Milo Jellick's store last evening on the pretence of asking for Hayfork's mail, but whose real interest was that he'd shown in Haskell himself. This was the one Milo Jellick named as Stack Coulter.

Right now, Coulter's face was blankly empty of all muscular expression, but a trapped uneasiness in his shadowed eyes told of his inner uncertainty. A small swelling pulled at a corner of his tight lipped mouth, and there was a solid bruise high up on the side of his head.

Haskell's tone softened to a slurring half-murmur, but there was no lessening of the chill in the fixed intensity of his glance.

"Mister, by all the signs, somebody branded you with a fist not too long ago. Maybe I did!"

Joe Peele, though thoroughly shaken up, struggled to a sitting position and cried in agreement.

"You did! You branded him. That's Stack Coulter. He was with Tendler and the rest when they ganged you last night. I hope you kill him!"

"Well now, Joe, that might be just a little extreme." Haskell's tone was still soft and half slurred. "On the other hand, something like this—!"

While speaking, he had moved a step or two closer to Coulter. He lowered the hammer of his rifle and

59

now, crouching swiftly, laid the weapon on the ground. Then, straightening, he sent a slashing fist out in a long, reaching blow.

It was almost too long, for Coulter saw it coming and partially dodged it. Even so, though landing glancingly, it had enough behind it to stagger him and spin him half around. Before he could recover, Haskell had moved in and hit him twice in his wide open flank. These blows brought Coulter doubling over, and Haskell, coming up on his toes to get full power into it, laid a driving fist on that narrow, sagging jaw.

Coulter went to his knees, then fell over on his side, pawing at his gun with a dazed clumsiness. Haskell jerked the weapon away from him, jacked the cartridges from it and scattered them across the street's dust with a backhanded toss. The gun he dropped beside its owner.

Joe Peele, on his feet now, came unsteadily up beside Haskell and peered down at the prone Hayfork rider, his face twisted, his voice shrill.

"Why don't you put the boots to him like he did to you last night? Dragging me that way—like I was some damned animal on the end of a rope . . . !" Joe drew back one scuffed, run-over boot.

"No!" ordered Haskell sharply. "None of that, Joe. Last night, when you ran him and his friends off with your old shotgun, you were the biggest man on this street. You kick him now, you're right down in his class."

"But dragging me that way—that's making a dog out of a man. That's like—like being horse-whipped."

"Depends on why he set out to drag you," Haskell soothed. "Now if it was just for sport, that would have been pretty mean, all right. But if he was set to get even for last night—which I figure he was, that's different. He wasn't just out to make mock of you, Joe."

60

"Mebbe you're right," Joe mumbled, quieting. "Mebbe that's it. But it won't ever happen again, by God! for I've taken my last pushin' around in this damn town, by Coulter or anybody else. From now on, my old Greener gun goes with me wherever I go. And I turn it loose on the first man who sets out to rough me!"

Saying which, Joe Peele started off, then paused and turned and said simply:

"I'm thankin' you again, of course. You're the best man to hit this town in I don't know when, Deputy."

Moving to recover his rifle, Haskell discovered stirrings all along the street. The sound of the shot had brought them out. Milo Jellick was on the porch of his store, watching intently, while Art Oren peered in heavy sullenness from the door of the Canyon House. An upstairs window of the hotel framed the startled anxious face of the girl, Ruby, and Amos Potter, just swinging down the hotel steps, came swiftly toward Haskell, his expression taut with concern. This lessened as Coulter, blinking and shaking his head, climbed shakily to his feet.

"That shot?" Potter asked.

"Mine," Haskell said briefly. "And high—on purpose. But if he hadn't let go of Joe Peele, the next one would have hit something. I'll see no man dragged and do nothing about it."

"He could have dragged a better man," Potter stated.

"There I'll argue with you." Haskell was bluntly harsh. "Joe Peele's got every right to walk this street without being mauled by this fellow Coulter—or by anyone else. And I'm not at all sure Joe Peele isn't the biggest man I've so far met in these parts. At least he's not afraid to stand up and be counted; which is more than I can say for certain others who crawl and side-

61

step and play it close to their vests, like they were trying to hide something. Now you come tearing out here full of concern for this fellow Coulter. Maybe there's a point you want to argue?"

Amos Potter shook his head with a sort of weary resignation.

"No, I don't want to argue. You can believe it or not, but my concern was for you, not for Coulter. There are things—you don't understand." He turned and went back to the hotel.

Haskell stared after him, puzzled and frowning. What was this talk about something he did not understand? Right now he had no slightest idea. He shrugged and put his attention on Coulter again, nudging Coulter's gun with his toe.

"Yours. Pick it up. And here's a word to take to your boss and the rest of the crew. Joe Peele is my good friend. He's to be left alone—strictly! Now—get the hell out of here!"

Leaning to recover his gun, Stack Coulter came near falling on his face, for the rubber was still in his legs and his eyes a trifle glassy. He made no answer to Haskell's warning words, just pulled slowly up into his saddle and reined away, leaving town without further stop.

Rifle across his arm, Haskell tramped on to the feed stable. In the runway of this a gaunt, roan-headed man met him, made swift appraisal, then nodded and spoke dryly.

"So 'tis you who are to blame. Now that I might have guessed."

Haskell stared. "Blame! For what?"

Faint humor crinkled a pair of blue, Irish eyes.

"For why Jim Kineen is missing a roustabout from his stable this mornin'. Yesterday I had one, but today the felly is gone, having up and dragged foot during

62

the night. Now I'm obliged to do me own work. When I hired that one my thought was that he was a bit off-color. Sure and this proves it. For when he saw you, his conscience began to hurt."

"You're speaking of the dirty one, the one who smelled?" Haskell asked, seeing in this gaunt Irishman with the twinkly eyes another man he might like.

"Now that you mention it, he was a bit foul," was the nodded rejoinder.

"When he saw me I wasn't wearing the star," Haskell protested.

Jim Kineen wagged his head, making in substance the same observation as had Milo Jellick.

"Ay—you were not. But you were wearing a certain look in your eye and swing to your shoulders which tell much. Something a little, dirty, scared one like Tate Vann would be noting at a glance. And so is gone. And had he seen the way you handled Coulter just now, he'd be going even faster and further. Do you mind my saying I like the treatment you gave Stack Coulter? The man has always been something of a bully, so it was a satisfaction in seeing him get his ears cuffed down. You'll be wantin' your horse?"

"That's right. Bring it out and I'll saddle up."

"That you will not!" differed Jim Kineen vehemently. "I will get the dun and I will saddle it. 'Tis a service you bought when you left the horse in this stable."

Haskell could make no complaint with the way the dun had been cared for. It was full fed, rested, curried and brushed down. When Kineen led it into the runway it pricked its ears and whickered softly at Haskell.

"Now there, friend, is a mark in your favor," exclaimed Kineen. "A ridin' animal glad to see its mas-

63

ter. Proof that it has known proper kindness and care."

Kineen spread the saddle blanket smoothly and dropped the saddle exactly in place with the first toss. He hooked the near stirrup on the saddle horn, caught the swinging cinch, and with head half hidden under the upflung stirrup fender, threaded the latigo and began setting up. Thus engrossed, he spoke carefully.

"You're lookin' for somebody in these hills—somebody special?"

With the hope that it might startle an enlightening answer, Haskell returned quick reply.

"Two of them. A Frank Gentile and a Jack Breedon. Like me, Breedon was a deputy."

"Ah, yes," murmured Kineen. "That Gentile felly. Sure and he rides with Rutt Dubison, who should be ashamed of the fact. For Gentile," he went on with a rising vehemence, "is a no-good, a bad one, a damned brute. I think of the time when he'd been drinkin' and gamblin' all night. He'd lost much and his temper was vile when he came out into the clean sunlight of a new day. He threw his viciousness at his horse, which he'd left standin' the night through at the Canyon House rail. He ended up beating the poor beast about the head with the butt of a loaded quirt until he'd blinded it. The animal had to be shot. I'm telling you it was a wicked thing! And had I a gun handy that day, then I'm thinkin' Frank Gentile would have been shot, too. For I've no time at all for any man who mistreats a dumb and helpless animal."

Kineen straightened as he spoke, the fires of an old and recurring anger bright burning in his eyes. "Ay," he repeated, "if I had a gun that day, then I would have used it."

"Gentile will end up strung on a slug or a rope,"

Haskell assured. "His kind always does. But Jack Breedon—what do you know about him?"

"Why," declared Kineen with a swift blandness, "there is one I never heard of before."

Haskell slid his rifle into its scabbard, gathered the dun's reins and stepped into the saddle. While the dun was being saddled he had built a cigarette. Now he paused to light this, looking down at Kineen over cupped hands.

"This town," he observed with considerable irony, "houses some of the damndest liars I ever met up with. Either the whole town is guilty of something or it is trying to cover up for someone who is. Before I'm done, I'll find out which. When I do, then will a strong brand of hell begin to fume. And that, my friend, you may count on!"

He stirred the dun to movement and rode out into the street.

Leaving town, he crossed the bridge and shortly thereafter took the cut-off which angled deeper into the hills. Here he let the dun set its own pace through a climbing tunnel of timber in which night's crisp breath and damp flavors still lingered. He rode with some wariness, for fresh hoof-prints, clear marked in the dew darkened dust, told that Stack Coulter had come and gone this way; in fact having passed so lately that a pine squirrel, once startled, only now had mustered courage to again explore the possibilities of a ripe seed cone lying beside the road. Disturbed this second time by a rider's presence, the small furred fellow scuttled to a tree top and from this lofty eminence soundly cursed Haskell and the dun.

Haskell smiled briefly at the squirrel's fretful scolding, then dropped back into his thoughts again, reviewing the various reactions he had met with. There was plainly no mystery about Frank Gentile, no reluctance to give an opinion or to talk about him. In this, both Milo Jellick and Jim Kineen had spoken freely.

Mention of Jack Breedon, however, brought an entirely opposite response. Jellick bluntly dropping all discussion, while Jim Kineen blandly denied ever having heard of Breedon. In Haskell's judgment, both Jellick and Kineen were sound men, as was Amos Potter, whose manner and words were equally puzzling. Then why the evasiveness at the mention of Jack Breedon's name?

Also, what about Katherine Levening's attempt to search his saddlebags, and later, the brutal mauling given him by Vince Tendler and the Hayfork outfit?

Questions—questions! And no sound answers.

Except, perhaps, for the cause of last night's beating. That, he reflected ruefully, was probably the price he'd paid for giving way to a completely normal impulse and kissing a pretty girl he caught about to rifle his belongings. Even though later, she had cried her denial of this.

Who to believe—what to believe?

Mainly, he decided grimly, only that which his own eyes and ears and cold judgment brought to him. He would ride and he would look and he would listen, and make his own rules to fit whatever situation cropped up.

The road climbed wooded slopes, circled a ridge point, climbed again and came out on the long-running spine of the ridge, where little glades and meadows broke through on either hand. There was a stir of motion at the timbered edge of one of these, and a rider showed, swinging out into the road to face him.

Katherine Levening.

Reined up, she watched Haskell with a grave intentness. On his part, Haskell swung a searching glance all about before he settled back in his saddle, touched his hat and acknowledged her presence with sardonic dryness.

"We meet it seems, here, there and yonder. Under circumstances which might be called peculiar. Fate, do you think, or design?"

She colored, but her answer came steadily.

"I thought you might ride this way."

"Not long ago someone else did, too. A rather rough bucko, Coulter by name. Now would he be somewhere close around?"

"No. He went by a good quarter of an hour ago."

"He didn't see you?"

She shook her head. "I was in the timber."

"Waiting for me?"

"Yes."

"Why?"

She did not answer immediately, but looked off across the clearing, sober and subdued. About her there was a hint of strain and weariness, yet she sat straight-backed in her saddle, a rounded, supple figure. Morning's sun, breaking down past the timber tops, laid a fan of light across her face, powdering the smoothness of her cheeks to a golden brown. Beneath slightly frowning brows her eyes were of the deepest blue.

Her glance came back to him.

"Why was I waiting for you? Because though I felt you would show, I was hoping you wouldn't; hoping—well—that you weren't real. Which sounds entirely ridiculous, doesn't it?"

"In one way, yes—in another, no." The dryness of Haskell's tone held on. "However, since last night, nothing really surprises me."

She knew what he meant. Bruises were a lingering dark stain under the weathered bronze of his face.

"I had nothing to do with that affair."

"So you say. But I saw your Hayfork foreman, Tendler, meet you at the hotel. And after that it was he and your Hayfork outfit that laid for me and worked me over."

She flared a little. "Not by any order of mine. I have told no one of—of exactly what took place in your hotel room."

"Yet you were ready to kill me," Haskell reminded. "At least so you said. You were wishing for a gun."

"Quite naturally I was furious. I had a right to be."

"I think I had a reason to be a little concerned, myself," Haskell drawled.

The slight surge of stormy feeling had darkened her eyes. She was, he thought, very fair to look upon. His tone turned milder.

"Just what did you expect to find in my saddlebags?"

She glanced at the star on his shirt, seemed about to answer, but ended by shrugging and saying nothing. He tried another angle.

"You say you did not tell Tendler about our little argument in my room. Maybe you've another idea why I had to receipt for a beating?"

Again that silent, enigmatic shrug.

"Worst country I ever saw for people to suddenly lose all power of speech," Haskell said with some sarcasm. Then he added, "Well, I could have done without the beating, and before I'm through there'll be those who'll wish they had no hand in it. As for the affair in my room, I'm not mad over that at all. Because it did have one very pleasant moment."

Strong color rushed across her face. Her shoulders stiffened and the old high pride came storming through.

"I certainly don't recall any!"

The retort was charged with a scorn so abrupt and cutting, it made Haskell redden and squirm a trifle.

"You pack a sharp spur, Katie Levening," he admitted wryly. "Still, I say it again. For me, it was a good moment!"

He brought Durham from a shirt pocket, creased a brown paper carefully and spun up a cigarette. He lit this and relished the first deep drag of tangy smoke.

Round about, as the sun climbed, the world was warming, and the resin breath of the timber came in on a little wind. Back along the road the squirrel still scolded, and a timber jay, swooping across the clearing on swift, soft wings, was a mote of glinting sapphire. Past the up-curling smoke of his cigarette, Haskell spoke again, not ungently.

"So now you know I'm real, and that I carry the star. What's the next move, Katie Levening?"

Again he glimpsed that hint of weariness in her, a weariness of the spirit as well as of the flesh. It dulled her expression somewhat, took some of the freshness from her face, and put a slight droop to the proud shoulders. When she spoke, it was in a low, uncertain way, as though to herself, rather than to him.

"I seem to have played the fool again. I don't know why I thought it might be different."

She lifted her reins, swung her horse away at a run. Haskell watched her flash into the timber and disappear. He stayed as he was while he smoked his cigarette down to a cold stub.

Finally he went on, reading hoof sign in the dust. Stack Coulter had covered this stretch at a jog. But Katherine Levening had held to a gallop for a good half mile, then hauled to a plunging halt, here joined by a third rider. After which the pair of them had gone on at only a slightly milder pace.

Within another half mile the road forked, as though

it had been forcibly split by the steadily lifting and sharpening rock spine of the ridge. By the hoof sign, all ahead had taken the left hand fork.

Once more reined up, Grady Haskell pondered matters. His initial thought on leaving town had been merely to quietly prowl some of this hill country, to ride high, for a man had to get up high if he wanted to see far. He had no intention of seeking out anyone directly; this was to be a ride to reconnoiter, to get some idea of the lay of the land.

But along the way he had met up with Katherine Levening, and the fact of her presence, her open admission as to why she had been there, her subsequent manner and the things she had said—and left unsaid—all told of an unease, a worry, and, though it was with a definite reluctance that he considered it, a strong suggestion of some sort of guilt.

Which was, he decided soberly, an angle demanding deeper investigation, and what more logical spot to start such investigation than Hayfork headquarters?

It was fairly obvious the girl had been heading home, so now Haskell started his horse into the left road fork. Immediately he set the dun up sharply. For, from the rocky lift of the ridge, a rifle flung down its thin report and a bullet gouged the road, chewing up a spatter of dust.

First impulse was to dodge into the timber, to get out of sight. But it was a thought Haskell stifled even as it began taking form. For had that bullet been so intended, it would certainly have slugged him out of the saddle, for he was a fair, open and easy target. The shot must have been a warning. Of what?

That the road was barred to him? There was a quick way to find out. He took it. He reined the dun ahead again. And again the rifle snarled, up there among the rocks, and again a bullet thudded into the road.

Haskell hauled back, cold anger climbing in him. He stared at the tangle of rock and timber above. No move there, no sound. Nothing to be seen except the gray, basaltic bones of the ridge, with solitary spikes of timber lifting here and there. Maybe a man could circle, climb higher up and come down on that hidden rifle from above. . . .

Impulse to try something of the sort surged in Haskell, but cold reason told him it wouldn't do. The hidden one already held the advantage of height, and in addition was almost certain to be familiar with every foot of this hill country. And you didn't, reasoned Haskell grimly, stand much chance of out-maneuvering a man in his own back yard.

A third bullet slammed into the road, the report of the gun a pinched echo spiraling up into the sun-warmed sky. Came a fourth bullet, striking closer. Here was a language, written in gunsmoke, and unmistakable. Plainly it closed this road to Grady Haskell, ordering him to turn back.

It was a galling thing to have to obey. But obey he did, for the simple reason it was the only intelligent thing he could do. No sane man tried to get a busted flush against a pat hand. Instead, you waited for a fresh set of cards.

So he went back as he had come, back down the hill road where a pine squirrel still scolded, and a crested timber jay was a blue jewel in the sunlight. Anger rode with him, steadily growing, wiping out all sentiment and replacing it with a strain of ruthlessness. It was one thing to meet with, and to a degree tolerate evasion and secrecy. But it was something else entirely to find a road blocked to you by slashing rifle fire.

In town this morning, Joe Peele had cried that being dragged was almost as bad in its effect on a man, as being horsewhipped. Here was something to add to that, reflected Haskell bitterly. To be headed off and herded around by slugs from a hidden rifle, was fully as bad as what had happened to Joe Peele. Particularly when you wore the star, were a man of the law. It not only defied your authority, it ridiculed you, made you look and feel foolish. As though you were, in effect, no better than a four-footed critter to be herded about by a handful of thrown rocks.

Well, this was a game that had just started, and the rougher other men wrote their rules, vowed Haskell, the rougher he'd write his own. There was more than one way to dredge up an answer, more than one way to get people to talk. There was always the final ruthless tactic.

It was a thing which could turn friend against friend, neighbor against neighbor. It was entirely legitimate, though to a degree demeaning, appealing as it did to human cupidity and greed. Bluntly, it was blood money. But it got results.

Yes, it would be a strange thing indeed if promise of reward money didn't loosen up some tongues!

6

On his return to town, Grady Haskell found no one about the stable, so unsaddled and cared for the dun himself. After which he went along to the store where Jim Kineen was perched on the counter swapping idle talk with Milo Jellick. The stable owner considered Haskell shrewdly.

"Now I don't know why, but when you rode out of my place this mornin', it was my thought you were off for the day. Friend, you are soon back."

"Soon back," agreed Haskell with some curtness. He turned to Jellick. "Did I hear you right last evening—a stage is due through today?"

Nodding, Jellick glanced at the old wall clock. "In about an hour. Lays over long enough for noon grub and a team change."

"Seeing you handle the mail, you'll have what I want." Haskell rang a coin on the counter. "A pencil, some writing paper, and a couple of stamped envelopes."

Milo Jellick laid out the required articles and Haskell, gathering them up, headed for the hotel and his room.

In the store, Jim Kineen slowly spoke.

"Yon goes a man bound to bring a deal of misery to some folks, for he'll not be stopped short of what he came into these hills after. What d'you suppose he met with back in the timber to put the extra cold look in his eye?"

Jellick shook his head. "I wouldn't know. But I do see a broad streak of toughness in him."

"Now there," Kineen observed, with a touch of dry humor, "I'm sure Stack Coulter would agree. You saw him handle Coulter?"

"I saw. And quick and wicked he was about it. Now I'm wondering what will happen the first time he and Rutt Dubison come together. You know how Dubison feels about any man with a star?"

"I know. Rutt's a wild one, keeping company I do not care for. Me, I'm thinking of the next meeting of Haskell and Vince Tendler. Coulter was one who helped gang Haskell last night, but it was Tendler who led the affair, which Haskell must well know." In sober thought Jim Kineen considered a moment, then shook a regretful head.

"Ay," he went on, "friend Haskell brings misery with him. But it is a thing that was bound to come, as the two of us have long known it would. I've a doubt, Milo Jellick, we've been smart, you and I, in refusing to answer him straight in his questions. It could be we've hurt matters more than we've helped."

"Yes, it could," Jellick admitted. "But sometimes the only refuge a decently honorable man has is in his silence. And if I must hurt a friend, I would rather it be by my saying nothing, instead of by saying too much."

"Which some might call splitting a pretty fine hair," mused Kineen, nodding. "Yet I am inclined to agree with you. In any case, what is done, is done. And we can but sit back and see what comes of it."

In his room, Grady Haskell cleared off the wash stand, spread his letter writing materials, pulled up a chair and set to work. To get things down exactly as he wished them to read took more time than he imagined, and he was just sealing the envelope when the dinner gong set up its mellow call.

Outside lifted the jangle of traces and the clack and squeal of dried out wheels. A glance from the window showed a dust covered stage and sweating team of six moving slowly along the street. Haskell hurried down and across to the store, where Milo Jellick was making up a meager sack of mail. Haskell handed over his letter.

"Put this one in there, too."

He turned to leave, then paused. "Where does the stage drop the mail?"

"Same place it picks up the incoming," Jellick answered. "Brandy Junction, on the railroad." Wielding an ancient cancellation stamp on Haskell's letter, he glanced at the address. "If," he added dryly, "you're wondering when you can expect an answer from Bill Hoe, it'll depend on how quick he gets one out. If right away, you should have it about this time come Friday."

He dumped the letter into the sack.

"Good part of a week away, eh?" pondered Haskell. "Well, that'll give me a chance to catch up on my sleep."

In the hotel dining room he took the same small wall table, and now it was the girl, Ruby, who brought him his food. That morning, from the upstairs window, she had seen him bring Stack Coulter to heel with a quick and savage ruthlessness, and the incident had made him big in her young eyes. Now her shy, half eager manner wrung a shadowed smile from him.

"Sure is something," he drawled, teasing, "having a pretty girl tidy up your room and then wait on you at meal time."

She flushed. "I—I wanted a chance to tell you how glad I was to see you knock that Stack Coulter down."

Haskell cocked an eyebrow. "So-o! Why would that be?"

The heat in her cheeks deepened. "Because—well, because my father—I mean, because I'm just—Ruby, he acts—oh, you know—"

"Yeah," murmured Haskell, "I think I know. Next time I meet up with Mister Coulter, maybe I'll knock him down again. Now, what were you going to say about your father?"

She appeared not to hear this, but hurried off and did not come near him again.

An after meal cigar fragrant between his teeth, Haskell stood on the hotel porch and watched the stage, a fresh team in the traces, roll out of town. After which he went along to the Canyon House, looked in, did not see who he wanted, so turned into the street again and sauntered back to the store. Here he stood quietly aside until a housewife with a big eyed baby on her arm, finished dickering with Milo Jellick over a basket of groceries. When she had gone, Haskell asked his question.

"Where might I find Joe Peel about now?"

"Depends," Jellick answered. "If he's managed to scrape up a pint somewhere, you could find him sprawled in most any odd corner, sleeping it off. But if he's had to stay reasonably sober for a change, then he'll probably be hanging around his shanty, nursing the shakes."

"Where is this shanty?" Haskell queried.

"Over on the river bank, north of town. Stands by itself. You can't miss it." Speculation narrowed Milo Jellick's eyes. "I suppose it's none of my business what you want the town drunk for, but I'm wondering."

"Why," said Haskell, speaking crisply, "it's like this.

76

Last night a crowd of eager buckos had me down in the dust of the street, doing their merry damndest to kick my ribs in and my brains out. And who was it put a stop to that bit of joyful business? Not any of the sober, respectable citizens of this damn town. No, indeed! It was just Joe Peele, the town drunk as you call him, who stepped in. So, from now on, drunk or sober, Joe Peele is my good friend. And I like to visit with my friends."

There was a sarcasm in these words which built a dull flush in Milo Jellick's round cheeks. "That," he said quietly, "was throwing it a little rough, Haskell. We couldn't all happen to be handy. I was in my living quarters out back. And as I've told you, I heard nothing of it, knew nothing of it until it was all over."

His tone mollifying, Haskell said, "Didn't set out to rawhide you. I just want to see Joe Peele accepted for what he is, a pretty good man."

"He'll be accepted for exactly what he proves himself worth," Jellick said curtly. "Up to now that's been damn little."

"Maybe so," retorted Haskell. "But last night he stood pretty tall and wide, out there in the street."

He left, circling through the alley between the store and the Canyon House, then on across a considerable interval to the river bank, where a raw boarded cabin crouched, gray with age and weather. Joe Peele sat on a bench by the open door. He got to his feet, a little awkward and self-conscious, as Haskell approached.

"Can't remember when I last had a visitor," he said. "Come on in."

On his part, Haskell knew a measure of surprise, too. For Joe Peele was clean shaven, and while the shirt he had on was badly wrinkled, it was clean. Also, the interior of this mean little cabin smelled of hot water and damp wood. It had been thoroughly scrubbed, walls and floor and ancient table top. Joe Peele did not miss Haskell's observant glance.

"I'd have done a better job of swamping out if I'd had a bar of lye soap. Man's in a hell of a fix, ain't he, when he can't even raise the price of a bar of soap?"

Knowing that an answer to this would be more embarrassing than would silence, Haskell said nothing, instead stepped over and picked up the sawed-off, double barrelled shotgun that lay on the bunk in the far corner of the room.

A glance told him that here was a high grade weapon, which, though worn and shiny from long use and handling, was in perfect shape, showing not a speck of rust or of any other kind of neglect. He balanced the gun in his hands.

"Considerable of a persuader, this," he said. "No wonder that crowd cooled off last night in front of it. You've had it a long time, Joe?"

"Nigh on to thirty years. Packed it regular when I was riding shotgun guard on the Harper & Sharpe stages between Gold Run and Bonanza City."

"And you've kept it ever since. Any special reason?"

Joe Peele squared his thin shoulders. "I figure it's like this. Every man has got to have something to hang on to in life. With me it's the old Greener, because it keeps reminding me that once I rated up as man-sized to a lot of people. Times I've wanted a drink of whiskey so bad I didn't know which way to turn. All I had to do to get the price of a bottle was sell the old gun. But I wouldn't do it. And times I could hardly stay on my feet, I needed food that bad. Selling the old Greener would have got me grub. Still I wouldn't sell it. I've always felt if I let go of the gun, then I wouldn't last no time at all. Guess that sounds kinda foolish to you?"

"Not at all," Haskell told him soberly. "It makes the best of sense. They were great days when you rode shotgun guard?"

"Great days?" A gleam came into Joe Peele's faded eyes and a touch of color warmed his gaunt, seamed cheeks. "The best! I wasn't just Joe Peele, the town drunk, then. Instead, I was Joe Peele, shotgun guard on as dangerous a stage run as the west ever saw. Yes, sir—shotgun guard, and prime target of every holdup man in the territory.

"Not many wanted the job. Curly Carr tried it, but lost his nerve after Mike Lyons was killed. Then there was Tod Wiley and Johnny Price, they both got it in holdups. Toward the end there was just Steve Allard and me left. Only reason Steve and me lasted, I guess, was because we were so damned young and reckless, having the luck of such—and because we shot first and asked questions after.

"Steve, he killed Rufe Jackson, who was plenty mean, while I did for Blackie Stent and winged Peck Yandle so bad he finally crawled into Gold Run on his own, looking for a doctor. He found the doctor all right, but too late to do him any good. The buckshot in him were too many and too deep; buckshot out of that gun you're holding. So, I got credit for wiping out two of the very worst, Blackie Stent and Peck Yandle.

"But nobody's good luck lasts forever. Somebody picked off Steve Allard from the aspens. They didn't try and stop the stage, they just pulled down on Steve and killed him from ambush. It never was found out for certain who did it, but the main guess was Pete Jackson, Rufe's younger brother, evening up for Rufe. So, finally, there was just Joe Peele left, riding shotgun."

He paused, lost in recollection, a man reliving the good, vital days of his life, with all their rich and fierce triumphs, but also remembering the tragic moments which could never be recalled and shaped to better ends. His fingers searched absently at the pocket of his shirt, an empty pocket. Haskell tossed a sack of Durham on the table top.

"Keep it, Joe. I got more."

Joe Peele built a careful cigarette, lit it and inhaled hungrily before going on.

"I should have quit that job the day Steve Allard was killed. Maybe, if I'd had real good sense, I'd never have signed on with Harper & Sharpe in the first place. For I had a wife and baby who needed looking after. But there was something about the danger of the job that got hold of a man. Besides, I was a big one in Gold Run and Bonanza City. I was the last of the Harper & Sharpe shotgun guards. I was riding stages stained for all time with the blood of half a dozen other men, good men who had died in line of duty. Yeah, I was somebody, and I gloried in it. And let it make an everlasting fool of me.

"For men liked to be seen with me along the streets and in the deadfalls. They wanted to buy me drinks, too many of them. I started gambling. Instead of staying home with my family of nights, I took to spending my time in the deadfalls, mixing whiskey with poker chips. Then came my final ride.

"I'd gambled all night and taken on more than my share of whiskey. Herb Averill was stage whip, that trip. Herb was the oldest and best driver Harper & Sharpe had. It was a dry run, no passengers. The bandits hit us at Steamboat Flat.

"And what was I doing when they did? Instead of being wide awake and on the job, ready to protect my driver and the treasure box, I was stretched out on top of the stage, sound asleep. A skin full of liquor and no rest at all the night before, saw to that. Herb—good old Herb Averill, he was letting me sleep it off. Now he tried to whip up and bust through, and they shot him dead.

"When Herb dropped the team swung wide, hooked a wheel on a stump at the side of the road, near upset the stage. I rolled off and bounced my head on the stump, which opened up a damned good cut and knocked me stiff. Lying there, bloody and still, I guess the holdups figgered they'd killed me, too, for they just cleaned out the treasure box and hauled foot.

"Later, some miners came along and found things as they were. Herb Averill was dead, a bullet through his heart. I was alive and full of whiskey, and lying on the gun I should have used on the bandits, a gun that hadn't even been fired. Those were the facts and the story they took back to Gold Run."

Again Joe Peele went silent, sucking his cigarette down to a last fragment, then crumbling it between his fingers.

"That was the finish," he said simply. "No longer was I Joe Peele, the big, brave shotgun guard. Instead, I was the worthless bastard who let my driver be killed and the treasure box looted, without putting up a fight or firing a shot. I was either a coward or a stupid drunk, or both. There was even talk that I'd made a deal with the holdup crowd, having lost so much gambling I was willing to sell out them who had trusted me and paid me wages. Harper & Sharpe may have believed this, for they fired me.

"What did I do? What plenty of damn fools have done before and since. I tried to hide in a whiskey bottle. When I finally sobered up, my world was shot to pieces. My wife and baby daughter were gone. Oh, I didn't blame Helen for leaving me; she had every right to, the way I'd been acting. Yet I set out to try and find her. I never did, down through a lot of lonely years, But I did find her grave.

"And got word of my daughter. Helen's half-sister was taking care of my girl. So I set out to run that trail down, and it led right here to Reservation. Maybe it would have been better for everybody if I'd headed the other way, or that I'd been killed the day Herb Averill was. For I ain't brought my girl Ruby anything to be proud of."

Haskell, a silent, intent listener, started slightly.

"Ruby! Would that be the girl at the hotel?"

Joe Peele nodded. "Jennie Wall, Helen's half-sister, looks after her. A mighty fine woman, Jennie Wall. Wish there was some way I could make up to her for all she's done for Ruby. I—I'd get me a job, if anybody would have me. I think maybe, if I had a job, I'd be able to stay away from the whiskey. It would give me reason to make a damn good try at it."

He came slightly around, to face Haskell directly.

"Thanks for listening to me. Don't know why I run on like I did. Just got started and couldn't seem to stop. But I sure feel the better for it."

"It does a man good to clear his mind," Haskell said.

"You've done a lot more for me than just givin' me a chance to clear my mind," Joe Peele declared. "Between last night and this morning, with what's happened because of you, a new feeling is stirring in me. I figger maybe I again got the right to hold my head up a mite."

Now did Haskell understand the shave, the clean shirt, the fresh scrubbed cabin. Here was a man reaching humbly for a shred of renewed self-respect.

"Joe, you got every right to hold your head up. You savvy horses?"

"Sure. Why?"

"Jim Kineen is needing a man around his stable."

"But Kineen wouldn't have me."

"I think he will."

A stir of eagerness grew in Joe Peele's eyes. "Maybe—if you asked him?"

"I'll ask him."

Haskell moved to the door, paused and turned.

"Six months ago a man by the name of Breedon came into this part of the country. Like me, he was a deputy out of Sheriff Bill Hoe's office in Ordeville. Did you ever see him, Joe—or meet him?"

Joe Peele hesitated, and when he did speak his words fell jerkily.

"I—saw him. I never—met him."

"You ever hear what became of him?"

The cabin had a single small window, which looked out and down across the river. It was open now, letting in the murmur of running water. Joe Peele stepped over and stood staring out of it. His voice ran low.

"I saw him a couple of times, then I never saw him again. I don't know what happened to him."

Haskell considered those thin, turned shoulders for a moment, then said crisply:

"Joe, you're lying."

Silent for a little time, Joe Peele shrugged. "That's right, I am." He came around, meeting and holding Haskell's glance. "I reckon there ain't many things I wouldn't be happy to do for you, everything considered. But the one thing I just can't do, is give you an honest answer to what you just asked me."

"Can't or won't, Joe?"

"Won't," said Joe simply. "Which I agree is poor reward for favors done. But it's the way things are. I hope you won't feel too hard against me."

Again Haskell considered him, face to face now. A thin, wry smile pulled at Haskell's lips.

"No, Joe—I won't feel hard about it. On the contrary, I admire you for your stand. And you know, Joe—I'm beginning to understand that someone in these parts can lay claim to the finest bunch of friends I ever heard of. Which doesn't make my chore any easier. But I got to go through with it. Now I'll go have a little talk with Jim Kineen."

He found Jim Kineen, pitchfork in hand, cleaning stalls and spreading new bedding straw. Leaning on his fork, the stable owner scrubbed a thin beading of sweat from his forehead and drawled mildly humorous words of accusation.

"I say it again. You are the cause of this, scaring off Tate Vann, so that I must now do me own stable chores. Have you come to mock me?"

Smiling faintly, Haskell shook his head. "To tell you I've found a man to take Tate Vann's place."

"And who would this be?"

"Joe Peele."

Jim Kineen grimaced open disgust. "That useless one?"

"Not useless. A good man."

"A hopeless drunk," retorted Kineen.

"Once, he was," Haskell corrected. "I just came from a talk with him. He's a man reaching desperately for another chance at respectability. He deserves one. You need a hostler, he needs a job."

"Friend, there are things you don't know about Joe Peele."

"I know all about Joe Peele. He told me the entire story, not sparing himself. I say he deserves a chance."

Jim Kineen eyed Haskell gravely.

"Now you are a bit hard to figure. I have seen a blazing ruthlessness in you, a savagery, even a cruelty when aroused, for there was no mercy in you this morning when you stunned Stack Coulter. Yet you would stand before me now, pleading the cause of a worthless derelict who would never draw another sober breath if some one would supply the whiskey. No, I do not understand you."

Haskell shrugged. "That part doesn't matter. What does is that Joe Peele gets another chance. Do me this favor, Jim Kineen. Take a walk out to his cabin. You'll find it still wet from a thorough scrubbing. And you'll find Joe fresh shaven and wearing a clean shirt."

"If that be so, then I admit to a gleam of hope," Kineen conceded reluctantly. "I will do as you ask. I will go and see."

"Fine! enthused Haskell. "I knew you were a fair and generous man."

"A sentimental fool, you mean," Kineen grumbled, putting his fork aside.

"He scrubbed the cabin with plain water," Haskell went on, "because he didn't have the price of a bar of soap. So I think a ten dollar advance in wages would help. And I'll make it good if Joe Peele doesn't work out every last cent."

"Now that makes us a pair of sentimental fools," growled Kineen. "And I will bet you another ten that he does not show up for work at all, but lies drunk somewhere about until the first ten is used up on whiskey alone."

"A bet I'll take," said Haskell quickly. "And make you another that you lose it."

Jim Kineen waved both arms about his head as he started for the street.

"Go 'long with you. You're like a swarm of gnats stinging at a man. You would talk me out of me last dollar, and I'll not listen any further."

7

SLOUCHED IN ONE of the several chairs scattered along the hotel porch, Grady Haskell watched another night muffle the town of Reservation in velvet folds. Supper was a half hour gone, and his after-meal cigar smoked to a stub.

Some life was stirring, an occasional shadowy figure crossing through a window's stabbing beam of light. A buckboard rattled the length of the street to a stop at Jellick's store. Shortly a pair of riders jogged by and made for the Canyon House. Out of the darkness Jim Kineen came drifting, to climb the hotel steps. He stopped and came around as Haskell's softly drawling words reached him.

"Well, do I owe you ten dollars, Jim?"

"You do not," growled Kineen. " 'Tis meself who owes you it and I have come to pay an honest bet."

Haskell smiled to himself. "You mean you've hired yourself a hand?"

"That I have." Kineen moved up beside Haskell's chair. "And one who is already at work this minute, cleaning and soaping harness by lantern light. So here is your money and it is a bet I am happy to lose."

"Also one I'll not collect on," Haskell said. "I was riding a sure thing, and knew it."

"You will take the money and no back talk," declared the stable owner. "It was a fair bet, fairly made."

87

"Nothing of the sort," Haskell differed. "If you must give the money to someone, give it to Milo Jellick and tell him to see Joe Peele gets some new jeans and a couple of shirts. Either that, or some food for his cabin shelf. It was damned empty when I saw it."

"Now there is a thought," agreed Kineen, "though Joe already has a bit of grub on hand now. And here is something which should interest you. After I'd seen Joe Peele and made our deal, I gave him the ten dollar advance and went to tell of it to Milo Jellick. But I also watched and wondered, with me fingers crossed.

"Soon Joe Peele came through the alley and turned right into the Canyon House, and all me fine feelin's went away and I says to meself—'Jim Kineen, you have been a great fool, while friend Haskell is another, for Joe Peele will not soon come out of the Canyon House, walking straight up and sober'. Yet he did, in less than a minute. And he came over to Milo Jellick's store and bought a few groceries. I could not understand it."

"Well, sir—when Joe left, I went straight into the Canyon House and asked Oren what had happened. Oren was fair bewildered. He said Joe Peele said he figgered he owed about ten dollars for free lunch he'd eaten, that he was going to pay it off a bit at a time and laid two dollars on the bar. Then he told Oren he'd not be drinkin' whiskey or eatin' free lunch any more. I tell you, Art Oren was a man not believin' his own ears."

"Art Oren," said Haskell briefly, "is a surly whelp. I don't like him. And from what I've seen of his free lunch it's no bargain at any price. I've a notion to go over there and make him give Joe back his two dollars."

"No, no!" exclaimed Kineen. "That would be hurting Joe, for he is paying off what he considers is an honorable debt. Leave well enough as is and be thankful it is so. And now I will get along and leave this money with Milo Jellick."

Kineen tramped off and Haskell tossed the butt of his cigar into the street and was considering lighting up another when Ruby Peele stepped from the hotel door, moved to the edge of the porch and there leaned against one of the posts of the overhang. She was entirely unaware of Haskell's presence.

Ruby Peele. Joe Peele's daughter. When he had talked to her earlier this day, Haskell reflected, she had refused to give her last name. Because, no doubt, her father was classed as the town drunk, and she knew a natural shame at this, and a persistent moodiness.

Over at Jellick's store Jim Kineen showed briefly as he turned in at the lighted doorway. Another figure came out, and, quick striding, angled across the street. Haskell clearly heard Ruby Peele's quick catch of startled breath and the soft gladness of her call.

"Neal—Neal Andrews!"

"Evening, Ruby," came the answering drawl. Then the speaker was up the steps and standing beside the girl in the light from the hotel door.

Here was a loose, rawhide leanness, clad in faded, ragged jeans and jumper and worn, battered boots. Here were thin, hard cheeks stained to a clean, ruddy bronze by wind and sun. Here quick, eager eyes and words and the same in reply.

"Oh, Neal—I was beginning to believe you'd forgotten the way to town."

"Now I darn near did," was the laughing answer. "Been kind of busy, fixing the cabin up so a lady might be willing to live in it. I got down to my last cup of beans, so I figured I'd better come in for some

89

supplies and a chance to visit my best girl. I started too late to be in time for supper."

"Which means you're hungry, of course?"

"Plumb wolfish. Even for kitchen leavings."

"Silly. There'll be much better than that. Come on."

They were gone then, hand in hand, leaving behind the bright echo of their young voices.

Grady Haskell lit his second cigar, slowly. Abruptly he knew the weight of the old aloneness. It came to him at times like this. It was a penalty of the profession. The star worked that way. It put a man off by himself. He had known many who had grown old in the service of the star. Some were married, had families. All knew many friends, else they could not have remained in office. Yet, married or single, in their quiet, introspective moments, all became solitary men, far off unto themselves, garbed in that cloak of aloneness.

Haskell had known the feeling even among friends of long standing. Here, among strangers it was doubly strong. For, while you might gain their respect, the liking of strangers came more slowly. To win respect for your star was vital, yet it was something that might be based on fear entirely, on naked animal fear. At best it was an opinion, coldly calculated. On the other hand, liking was an emotion, and carried warmth. And a man could yearn for some of that warmth.

It seemed he could still hear the trilling gladness in Ruby Peele's voice as she greeted that lanky youngster just now. When or where had he, Grady Haskell, ever known such glad greeting? His lips twisted in sudden bleakness. If ever, he could recall neither the time or the place. The last girl he had faced was one who had whip-sawed him with indignance and scorn.

Katherine Levening. . . .

He got to his feet, stirred to movement by the somber acid of his thoughts. He moved to the edge of the porch, paused there. The early dark of the street had thinned, star-glitter now spreading its pale, silver glow along the earth.

Sound came in from down street, the riffle of massed hoofs. Hoofs coming at a steady-paced walk, which fact somehow carried in it a hint of things ominous. Haskell dropped back into the deeper shadow of the porch and watched the dark flow of movement pass.

A lone rider was out ahead of the rest, a high, flat shape in the starlight. A full dozen others followed. Stir of soft movement beside him, jerked Haskell quickly around. It was Amos Potter who stood there and who now spoke murmuringly.

"They always come into town at that damned, measured walk, and it puts a cold finger up and down a man's spine. You're looking at Rutt Dubison and the Beaverhead crowd, Haskell. Some bad ones out there—some real bad ones. There won't be many of the town regulars stirring around tonight."

"You mean," Haskell demanded, "that a decent citizen might be afraid to move about in his own town just because this Dubison hombre and a few wild ones have ridden in?"

"Yes and no. Call it having sense enough to steer clear of possible trouble by staying off the street for the night."

"Amounts to the same thing. And a hell of a note, too. I see they're hauling up at the Canyon House. I'm going to drop by and have a look at them."

"I wouldn't do it," Potter said quickly. "Some of that crowd—most of them, probably—are wanted, somewhere. They're bad ones. To them, that star of yours would be like a red flag to a bull."

Haskell swung his shoulders and spoke with a sudden harshness.

"The time ever comes, Potter, when I'm afraid to carry this star anywhere, that's when I take it off—for good! Bad ones, you say? Hell! I can get rough myself. Yes, I'm going to step into the Canyon House for some cigars."

Potter shrugged. "It's your skin. Don't say I didn't warn you."

"I won't," Haskell said. Then he added, with a touch of sarcasm, "though I wonder why you should."

The hotel owner had started to turn away, but now came back, half angry at the bite in Haskell's words.

"All right, I'll tell you why. It's because I'd begun to believe you were the kind of lawman I've hoped would show here in Reservation; one broad enough to know sympathy and understanding, and willing to admit that justice can sometimes be rendered truly, far from any recognized court of law."

"Interesting," said Haskell bluntly. "But if you're suggesting a soft streak in me, don't count on it. With me, duty comes ahead of everything."

"I don't mean softness," Potter said. "I mean what might be called a decent appreciation of facts."

There was little mirth in Haskell's laugh.

"Ah, yes—facts! Something I've been looking for since I rode into this town, but which all you righteous citizens hide like you might precious jewels. Show me a few of those facts to appreciate. Such as—what has become of a deputy sheriff named Jack Breedon? Did you ever see him? Do you know where he is?"

Amos Potter hesitated, held with a moment of indecision. Then, as he wheeled away, he murmured:

"I say again that to go into the Canyon House would be poor judgement on your part and not prove a thing. But if you must go, I wish you luck. You may need it."

Haskell stared across at the Canyon House, the bleakness of his mood deepening. An appreciation of facts, eh? Well, if that was what was needed, then others had better start showing some of it. For they couldn't be further wrong if they thought to go on forever blocking him and the authority he represented with their evasion and their lies. Or with warning rifle fire across a road, either!

With an abrupt gesture, he threw aside his half smoked cigar, dropped into the street and swiftly crossed. The horses at the Canyon House hitch rail had not yet settled to quietness after travel. They stamped and shifted and spread the warm reek of their sweat across the night. Starlight threw enough radiance to disclose a filled rifle scabbard on every saddle.

Haskell stiffened a hand against the swinging door of the saloon and drove it open far enough to enter, yet not to its fullest extent, for it was blocked by violent contact with a man's back. The owner of this came around in a gust of cursing.

He was lank and narrow jawed, badly scarred with pock marks, and with a quick, snarling anger thinning his lips across broken teeth. But as he glimpsed Haskell's star, the cursing ran out into a grunt of warning, and he gave back, staring.

"Better," Haskell said curtly. "You should know more than to block a busy doorway."

The bar was lined. Art Oren bustled heavily back and forth, pouring drinks, making change, fawning subservience in every move and look. At the rear of the room a gaunt rider sat in a tipped back chair and guardedly observed the newly arrived activity. This one Haskell recognized as the grizzled Hayfork hand, Sandy, who had been with Katherine Levening and Vince Tendler in the Rancheria Creek meadows yesterday morning, and who had later trailed him all across the hills to Reservation.

Along the bar the drone and clatter of words abruptly quieted, and a high, flat figure swung out of the press. Here a swarthy one, with cold, black eyes set on either side of a hungry beak of a nose. He laid narrow survey on Haskell, then nodded.

"Heard there was a new deputy in town. Me and the boys thought we'd ride in and get acquainted."

The words were fair enough, but to Haskell they carried the faint edge of an insolence.

"You'd be—Rutt Dubison?" he asked.

"That's right. Why? You been hearing things about me?"

"Some."

Rutt Dubison laughed, and it was a strangely disturbing one, being virtually soundless.

"This damn town! Full of squirming, spineless little bastards. They wouldn't dare talk up to my face. Well, you can see I'm just an ordinary two-legged man. And not a bad fellow at all. Which I'll prove to you now by buying you a drink. Hey, Oren—pour one for the deputy!"

Again Dubison's words were fair, but Haskell hesitated while he had another look at the room. Glances, guarded and wary, met his. Bad ones, these, so Amos Potter had warned. And Potter was right. These riders from the remote Beaverhead range wore the inescapable brand of their kind, a wildness indelibly stamped upon them; the wildness of the pack, running together at the moment for mutual benefit.

Coming away from Ordeville, Haskell had carried with him a mental picture of Frank Gentile, as furnished by Bill Hoe. Now, as he marked one after another of these men with swift scrutiny, he saw none who fitted Gentile's description. And, he mused, if word could so swiftly reach Rutt Dubison on the Beaverhead that a deputy was in Reservation, then it could also have reached Frank Gentile. In which case, at this very moment, Gentile might be riding fast and far to some new hideout.

Well, if that be so, it could not be helped. Primary concern, as Bill Hoe had emphasized, was still the strange disappearance of Jack Breedon. And it was possible that even here, among these wild ones, a judicious bit of questioning or a shrewdly dropped hint might turn up some definite word or lead. It was, Haskell decided, worth a try.

For he knew there was nothing more fallacious than any theory of honor among thieves. The primary concern of these men was wholly for themselves as individuals. No man was more self-centered and self-seeking than one of outlaw bent. Such was the very line of thought that made him an outlaw. So, in the cause of gain or individual welfare he could and would turn on another of his kind without mercy.

"Drinks are ready, Deputy," reminded Rutt Dubison. "We'll have this one together."

They made way for him at the bar. Moving up to it, the rub of a vague uneasiness stole through Haskell. Had there been a hint of sardonic mockery in Rutt Dubison's words, or was it that his imagination, because of Amos Potter's foreboding attitude, was beginning to run away with him?

Should he have stayed clear of the Canyon House this night, or had he, because of a somberness of mood occasioned by other cause, let reckless impulse push aside ordered judgment and so led him into something he'd been wise to have avoided?

He swung his shoulders slightly. What the hell! His gun hung at his hip and the badge of his authority was plain for all men to see and respect. Which was enough, any time, any place. And to back away from this thing now would finish him and his purpose in the Trinity Hills just as surely as if he lay dead on the floor.

He picked up his glass, raised it, looked at Rutt Dubison standing beside him.

"Luck!" he said.

"Luck!" Dubison echoed.

It was while the glass was at his lips and the whiskey burning in his throat that he felt the weight of his gun leave the holster. Beside him, Rutt Dubison exclaimed exultantly.

"All right—grab him! I got his gun. He was easy—just another star-toting fool, like I figured!"

Gagging on whiskey half swallowed, Haskell whirled. He managed to get around and half a stride free of the bar before being slammed back into it again and pinned there, a man hanging to each arm, a third driving a shoulder against his chest. And so they held him, helpless, while dismal anger and disgust flooded through him.

It had been so simply, so easily done! While he had his head tipped back, his nose in a whiskey glass, this Rutt Dubison—this high, mocking devil beside him, had lifted his gun with contemptuous ease. Fool, Dubison had called him. Fool was right—!

Wildness was rioting in Haskell, but he fought it back, knowing that any attempt to struggle free would be useless and guarantee him a beating. So he stood quietly, looking up at Rutt Dubison standing before him, a full half head taller. Dubison's mouth was twisted in jeering taunt, and his cold eyes were full of a sardonic mockery. Haskell managed to keep his words even.

"What's it all about, Dubison? This, I don't savvy."

"You will, you will," Rutt Dubison assured him.

"You know, Deputy, there's one big reason I never had any use for one of your kind. You're all alike, either crooked as snakes, or dumb as hell—which is worse. For while I can know some respect for a smart man, I hate to give even breathing room to a dumb one. Now you said you'd heard things about me. Then maybe you heard I don't want any of your kind around me. Bill Hoe should understand that by this time. So, minus your gun and your precious star, I'm sending you back to remind him again of that fact. Also, you can tell him that if he sends any more of your kind sniffing around, they'll go back in a box."

Reaching out, Dubison tore the star from Haskell's shirt and flipped it aside. He spoke again.

"I'll be in town again, Deputy. If you're still hanging around, then I really will make you hard to catch. Now—go ahead, boys—throw him out!"

This they did, literally. They rushed Haskell to the door, kicked it open and sent him stumbling headlong into the night. He slammed into the hitch rail, jackknifed over it, while horses reared and snorted above and around him.

Laughter mocked him from the saloon's open door, the sound raucous across the dark. Then the door swung shut and he was alone with his shame and a rage so black and destructive it filled his whiskey stung throat with the bitter phlegm of nausea. He straightened up, then hunched over the hitch rail again, actually physically sick, so violent were the fires of fury in him.

And the shame! It was worse than the rawhide lash of a whip, biting at him. Stupid, Rutt Dubison had called him—stupid and a fool. All of that, Grady Haskell—all of that! Played for the veriest sort of sucker, and gulping the bait. Stripped of gun and star and thrown bodily out of a deadfall to the tune of the scornful and contemptuous laughter of a pack of two-legged wolves. Why, they hadn't even shown him enough respect to kill him!

Again he was physically sick, his throat scorched with the raw bitterness of his own bile. He gagged and choked over this, then came erect once more, and turning, scrubbing the back of his hand across his fouled mouth. He'd lost his hat and his hair hung down over his eyes, which were afire with a malign savagery as he stared at the Canyon House door.

He stayed so for a long moment, then moved away, knowing exactly what he wanted and what he was going to do. He wheeled in between the Canyon House and Milo Jellick's store and went through this alley way at a hurrying pace that was just short of a run. Coming out into the interval north of town, he went on across this to the river bank where Joe Peele's cabin crouched, a low, dark shape in the star silvered night.

He tried the door, found it unlocked and stepped through. He knew the cabin would be empty, for Joe Peele was already at work in Jim Kineen's feed and livery stable. Haskell scratched a match and by its feeble glow found the lamp on the table and set this alight. After which he located Joe Peele's old sawed-off Greener shotgun, resting on a pair of wooden wall pegs at the head of the bunk.

He lifted the weapon down, looked for shells for it and found some in a cigar box on a shelf. He pocketed half a dozen of the lethal buckshot loads, broke the gun and slipped two more of these into the gaping, twin chambers. He closed the gun, blew out the lamp and headed into the night again. retracing his way across the interval and through the alley at the same bleakly purposeful driving pace. On the street once more he wheeled to face the door of the Canyon House.

Deliberately, first the left, then the right, he drew back the hammers of the Greener. Then, with the gun held hip-high and level, he moved to the door and with a driving kick sent it crashing open. He stepped through.

8

IF BEFORE THERE had been sound in the Canyon House, there was none now, save the thin sibilance of startled, indrawn breaths. Men who had been talking and laughing but a moment before were now suddenly voiceless, and with no mirth in them at all as they came around in one common movement to face Grady Haskell and the big Greener. With their first look, all but one were struck with a tense silence and a frozen immobility; all except the pockmarked one, he of the narrow jaw and broken teeth.

No man would guess, or would ever know, what desperate impulse drove this one to defy the bitter purpose in Grady Haskell's eyes and the massive threat of the Greener. Yet, something set the fellow off, there where he stood not two strides distant. With muttered imprecation he crouched and went for his gun.

Haskell swung the Greener and fired from the hip.

The room bulged with the hoarse roar of the big Greener, and the charge of buckshot, at this short range, literally picked the pock-marked one up and threw him back and dropped him, broken and twisted and instantly dead. Then the reeking Greener was menacing the room again, backed by Haskell's harsh words.

"That's how it will be again if anybody wants the other barrel!"

Had it been a revolver that Haskell held, or a rifle, they might have gambled and made a try for him. But not against that sawed-off terror. The Greener, at this short range, was too certain, too lethal, too full of a shattering, destructive wickedness. If they needed evidence of this, it lay there before them, something which, only short seconds before, had been an erect, living human being, but which now was just a shrunken, twisted heap. So they stared at the dead man, at Haskell and the Greener—and were still.

"Over against the wall!" Haskell gave the shotgun a little wave of direction. "Face it and put your hands against it—as high as you can reach. You, too," he told Art Oren.

Boot heels clumped, spurs scuffed, as they obeyed in a tense, careful shuffle. Oren, his heavy face flaccid and pallid, almost fell down in his clumsy eagerness to obey. From down the length of the room, Haskell met the eyes of Sandy, the grizzled Hayfork rider, and the old fellow spoke quietly.

"Not arguing, understand. Just wanting you to know I don't belong with this crowd. Fact is, I was figuring how to get clear of them without trouble, when you came in. That's the straight of it, Deputy."

Haskell considered him for a bleak moment, then nodded curtly.

"You can prove that by collecting their guns for me. But—watch yourself! I've had a bellyfull of fancy treatment in these damn hills, and I've little trust left for anybody around here. Go ahead—get their guns!"

Sandy obeyed with alacrity, stepping in behind the Beaverhead crowd, emptying holsters and piling the guns on the bar.

"Now outside," Haskell ordered. "Get their rifles."

Sandy made three trips, back and forth, before he

had all of these. Rutt Dubison looked across his shoulder at the old rider and spoke insolent threat.

"Lee, after this you can figure your time in these hills as run out. One of us will catch you along some trail, and that will be it!"

Haskell moved closer in. "Turn around, Dubison!"

Rutt Dubison obeyed, the barest flicker of uncertainty showing in his cold eyes.

Haskell looked him up and down.

"So you'd still make the big threat, still try to throw the bully-puss around. And you don't like lawmen because they're all crooks, all fools. From now on, you're going to send all like me back to Bill Hoe in a box. Hell, Dubison—maybe you figure you own these Trinity Hills, that they're all yours from end to end? Well, I don't believe it. To me, you just don't stand that high or that wide. And what you need is to be cut down to size—like this!"

Speaking, Grady Haskell's words had steadily increased in harshness. Now he swiftly reversed the Greener, swinging the muzzle back, shooting the heavy walnut butt out and up and ahead, smashing into Rutt Dubison's face. It was a calculated blow with no mercy in it, for, at this moment, there was no mercy in the man who delivered it.

Driven back against the wall, Dubison seemed to hang there, angular and strained. Then a great looseness ran through him and he fell forward and lay senseless on the floor.

Haskell stared down at him for a moment, then nudged the muzzle of the Greener against Art Oren's beefy back.

"Get a bucket of water and douse him with it!"

Oren brought the water from behind the bar, upended it on Dubison's head and shoulders. There was no immediate effect, but presently Dubison groaned and

103

rolled over on his back. The impact of the gun butt had done his face no good at all. A cut curved down his forehead from the hair line to the bridge of his nose, and both eyes were already swelled tight shut.

Haskell put his back to the bar, so that he might sweep the room with the threat of the Greener.

"All right," he told the balance of the Beaverhead crowd, "you're leaving, now. Get Dubison on his horse. Take that other one, too." His glance briefly touched the dead man.

Surly and dangerous, they did as they were told. A couple of them hoisted Dubison to his feet, led him stumbling and blindly weaving into the night. Others carried out the pock-marked one. The last one of the gang to leave paused short of the door and made sullen demand.

"What about our guns?"

"You haven't got any," Haskell told him coldly. "On your way!"

From the saloon doorway, Haskell watched as they tied a dead man across one saddle and boosted a weaving, half-conscious one into another. Then, a dark mass of men and horses, they wheeled away through the star glow into the obscurity of distance. And from that distance, beyond the far edge of town, a single yell drifted back, wild and hating and vengeful.

Haskell closed the door, turned back. Art Oren, with another bucket of water and a mop, came from behind the bar and set to work on the floor where the dead man had lain. He flashed a nervous glance at Haskell.

"Don't think I jibe with the things Rutt Dubison does, because I don't. It's just that bein' in business I can't afford to play no favorites."

"See that you stick to that," Haskell told him curtly. "Else you may find yourself riding the wrong horse."

The deep growl of the Greener's report had carried well beyond the walls of the Canyon House. It reached the ears of Jim Kineen and Milo Jellick in Jellick's store, and those of Amos Potter in the hotel. More faintly it came to Joe Peele, where he labored by lantern light over a tub of harness in Jim Kineen's stable. And it fetched all out for a look along the street, so that they saw the Beaverhead crowd wheel out of town and send back that furious, taunting yell. All of which hinted of strong happenings in the Canyon House and now brought these viewers hurrying.

Jim Kineen and Milo Jellick were the first to arrive, with Amos Potter but a few steps behind. Joe Peele was breathless when he burst in, for he had come at a run from the other end of town.

"That—that shot!" he blurted, panting. "I'd have swore it was my old Greener cutting loose. No rifle ever—"

"It was your Greener, Joe," broke in Haskell, unloading the gun. "I had to borrow it to put some smart ones in their place. Hope you don't mind?"

"Huh—hell, no!" puffed Joe. "Just so it got results."

Haskell handed the shotgun to its owner. "It got results." Tone and mood were turning somber with reaction.

Over in a far corner, lamp light picked up a metallic glint. It was Haskell's star, where Rutt Dubison had contemptuously flung it. Haskell recovered it, pinned it back in place. The room was silent and he felt the weight of every eye. He made a slow turn, met their various glances, then spoke with a deep grimness.

"Maybe, after a while, the idea will get around that

I didn't come into these hills just for the ride." He centered on Sandy Lee. "A little ago you said that all you wanted was to get clear of this place before Dubison and his outfit threw trouble your way. What was that supposed to mean? Why would they push trouble at you?"

The grizzled rider shrugged. "It's no secret that Hayfork and the Beaverhead crowd don't mix worth a damn. Had I known they were due to hit town tonight, I'd have been long gone by the time they arrived. But, all of a sudden, in they busted. Then you showed. After that—" Sandy shrugged again.

"Last night," Haskell said, "out there in the street I took a pretty mean roughing around by Hayfork riders. You have a hand in it?"

Reply was quick and emphatic. "I did not! I wasn't even in town last night."

"Yet, yesterday, you trailed me all the way in from Rancheria Creek?"

"That's right, I did," Sandy admitted steadily.

"After which you returned to headquarters with the word where I'd ended up—which was here in Reservation?"

"That's right," Sandy repeated. "But I didn't sit a saddle again until today."

Bleakly musing, Haskell searched through the scatter of weapons along the bar, found his own gun, checked and holstered it. Again he turned to Sandy Lee.

"Obliged for your help. But in your boots, after what Dubison said, I'd ride all trails pretty careful."

"Been doing that for some time," Sandy said dryly. "It's a habit that grows on a man in these hills. Now, if it's all the same to you—?"

Haskell nodded. "Sure. You can go along."

106

Sandy tramped out, and then hoofs made a fading murmur along the street.

Once again Haskell swung his glance. "Any more questions?"

Art Oren finished with his mop and bucket of water. Amos Potter eyed the freshly scrubbed area, then slowly spoke.

"When they rode out, there was one tied across his saddle. Which one?"

"I wouldn't know the name," Haskell said. "He tried to throw a gun under the direct threat of Joe Peele's Greener. I can regret the necessity a little, now. But at the time I was red-eyed."

"It was Rudy Shedd," supplied Art Oren heavily. "He didn't show no sense at all."

Jim Kineen was looking over the guns on the bar.

"Now here is a fine collection of hardware. Just what will you do with it, Haskell?"

"Turn it into scrap metal. You got a forge around your stable?"

"There's a small one out back, used to shoe a horse now and then."

"Good enough—I'll use it in the morning. Oren, you got some place where these guns will keep until then?"

"If I lock them in my liquor room they'll be safe enough."

"Lock them there." Haskell produced the shotgun shells he'd pocketed. "Here, Joe—I didn't need these. And I'll clean and oil the Greener."

Joe Peele shook his head. "I'll take care of it. And should you ever figure you need the old persuader again, you know where to find it."

Haskell dropped a hand on Joe's arm. "Thanks, my friend." After which he moved to the door, through it and out into the night.

107

The moment the door closed, Jim Kineen whirled on Art Oren. "All right—tell it! You were here, you saw it all. What the devil happened?"

The saloon owner told it, ending:

"And when Haskell came busting in the second time, near knocking my door off its hinges, with that shotgun level and ready, he looked nine feet high and twice that wide across the back. Then Rudy Shedd went loco or something, going for his gun. I never saw such a fool play. Hell! That shotgun blew him down like he was a weed in front of a high wind.

"Rutt Dubison didn't show good sense, either. He tried to rawhide Sandy Lee, threaten him. So Haskell gave Dubison the butt of the Greener square in the face, knocking him stiff. I tell you—right about then Mister Deputy Sheriff Haskell was as tough a customer as any I ever looked at in my time. And when that Beaverhead crowd left, they were a damn well cooled off bunch."

"For the present, perhaps," Milo Jellick observed soberly. "But they'll be back. Rutt Dubison won't take this without a try at getting even. He can't afford to—not and hold that wild gang with him."

"All that may be," Art Oren admitted. "But if I was in Rutt Dubison's boots I'd stay away—I'd stay far away. Yes, sir—far away!"

From the Canyon House, Grady Haskell had gone straight to the hotel and climbed to his room. Here he lit the lamp, unbuckled and hung his gunbelt on a bed post. His feeling was one of being strangely drained, or parched, with all his nerve ends raw and smarting. This, he decided bleakly, was the physical residue of the rage and the sickness the rage had occasioned. And some of that rage was still a fire in him, a banked fire now to be true, and buried far down. But still smoldering.

Last night this room had been sanctuary for bruised flesh, while tonight it was that for a bruised spirit. Just now, Haskell couldn't be sure which was the worst.

Seeking to relax, he doused his face in the wash basin, then rolled a cigarette and lay back on the bed, staring at the ceiling. It held a picture, that ceiling did, the picture of a man's face at the precise split second when shocked life left and violent death took over; the narrow, pock-marked face of the man Art Oren had named as Rudy Shedd. It wasn't a pleasant picture, and Haskell tried to get rid of it by closing his eyes. Which did no good. The picture remained.

Out in the hall a step sounded, followed by a knock on the door. A gust of irritation ran through Haskell.

"I'd rather be alone," he called harshly.

"Which is understandable," Amos Potter said, as he pushed open the door and stepped through. "And I'll leave you so after you get outside of this."

He carried a glass of whiskey, a big glass with four stiff fingers of liquor in it.

The irritation seeped out of Haskell. Here was a kindly, thoughtful gesture. He got to his feet, accepted the glass.

"Decent of you, Potter," he said gruffly. He added, with a ghost of a tired smile, "I'd call it a man-sized drink. Big enough to rock anybody to sleep."

"Which is what it's meant to do," Potter said.

Haskell put the drink away, pulling his lips thin across his teeth as he tensed against the fiery jolt. He caught his breath, let it out in a little exclamation.

"Hah! That sure was the bottom of the bottle!"

Potter took the empty glass and turned back to the door. He looked over his shoulder.

"For what it may be worth, so far as I know, Rudy Shedd never drew an honest breath in his life."

The door closed. Haskell dropped back on the edge

of the bed, pulled off his boots. The relaxing warmth of the liquor was all through him as he undressed. Within minutes the lamp was out and he was in the blankets and sound asleep.

The forge was a portable one, with a handle to turn to drive the blower. Also there was a short bench holding an anvil and a vise. Joe Peele was cranking the forge and the air draft hissed through a gather of red hot coals. From a burlap sack, Grady Haskell lifted a heavy revolver. He flipped open the loading gate, spun the cylinder and dropped fat, yellow cartridges from the chambers, one by one. The weapon fully unloaded, he thrust the barrel of it into the forge coals.

Joe Peele grunted and pointed to the walnut grip of the gun. Three notches had been carved in it.

"Feller who owned that one was either a bragging liar or a cold blooded whelp. Damn any man who notches a gun, I say. I don't care what he says or how he acts on the outside, way down deep in him somewhere is a rotten spot. A decent man does his best to forget them he'd had to smoke down, not notch a gun so he can remember better."

Soon the barrel of the revolver began to glow. Protecting his hand with a piece of burlap, Grady Haskell took hold of the butt of the gun, lifted it clear of the coals, put the end of the barrel in the vise and with a solid pull, bent the barrel at sharp right angles.

"There'll be no more notches cut in that one!"

He tossed the gun aside to cool and reached into the sack for another.

First rays of morning's sun were peering in past the low-sloping roof of the stable, yet were not high or strong enough to dissipate all of night's lingering chill, wherefore the warmth of the forge fire was welcome and its smoke a not unpleasant tang to the nostril. In a corral, several horses sought the sunniest corner and bunched there. A nearby manure pile steamed and all about hung the layered odors of the stable.

Haskell watched Joe Peele's thin figure swing back and forth as he cranked away at the forge, watched and marveled. For yesterday morning at just about this time, Joe Peele had been a huddled figure on a corner of Milo Jellick's store porch, a ragged, unkempt human derelict, shaken and wretched in his need for whiskey. Now he was a different man. In new jeans and shirt, clean shaven, a new light in his eyes and color in his gaunt cheeks, he was steady and full of industry. He seemed to feel Haskell's glance and to read the thoughts behind it, for he spoke gruffly.

"Yeah, I know. I'm not sure I understand it myself. Yesterday, around this time, whiskey was all I could think of. Now, to hell with it! It's a man's mind that makes him a souse. He's just what he thinks he is, no more, no less. Yesterday I wasn't worth a damn, to myself or anybody else. Today I'm of some use. And that's it—that's all of it, Grady. Being useful is the most important thing in all this world, I guess." He paused for a moment before adding, "This is the best day I've known since I don't know when. Mebbe, bye and bye, even Ruby won't be ashamed of me no more."

They kept steadily at it. Barrels of both revolver and rifles, every gun taken from the Beaverhead crowd, were heated and bent and ruined for any future use. Haskell had just thrown the last one aside to cool when Jim Kineen stepped through the stable's rear door. He eyed the results of their labors.

"Nothing there will ever shoot again," he observed dryly. "Just so much junk. What's with it now?"

111

"Into the river," Haskell said. "There's a deep hole just back of Joe's cabin."

"That will make it rather complete, won't it?"

"Damned complete! Which is what I want—with the word reaching Dubison and his Beaverhead crowd, as well as the rest of the country round about."

Pursing his lips, Jim Kineen nodded slowly.

"I believe I understand what you mean. The final emphasis of authority?"

"That's it," said Haskell briefly.

Joe Peele gathered up an armful of the ruined guns and set off toward the river with them. Jim Kineen gazed after him, gravely speculative.

"Grady Haskell, you've balanced the account—that you have!"

Puzzled, Haskell demanded: "How so?"

"Why," said Kineen, "though you left Rudy Shedd dead, you have brought Joe Peele alive. I wish it might stop there."

Haskell began spinning up a cigarette.

"Nothing stops until it's finished. My chore isn't!"

9

FROM THE CREST of a small benchland tucked against a wall of pine timber, the Hayfork headquarters looked down across a full mile of high mountain meadow. Ranch buildings were of logs, low built and sturdy, with stake-and-rider corral fences of split rails. Beyond buildings and corrals, along the edge of the pines, a thick fringe of aspens laid a belt of silver and pale gold color.

Out of the aspens a dripping, moss-covered wooden trough brought spring water to the ranch needs, then spilled steady excess of it down the slope to wander the length of the meadow in a small, brushed-over creek. A road curved into the meadow at its lower end, ran the full length of it, then climbed to headquarters. In scattered bunches, cattle bedded along the edge of the meadow or grazed across the face of it.

The pale smoke of early morning fires winnowed about the chimneys of the ranchhouse and the cookshack, and the rich, enticing flavors of coffee and bacon were adrift on the moist, chill air.

At the ranchhouse kitchen table Katherine Levening ate a solitary breakfast. In a simple red-and-white checked gingham dress, and with the dark luxury of her hair drawn smoothly back and held so by a bit of ribbon, she looked girlishly young and soberly wistful. For she had much to think of and worry about.

Rising and dressing early, she had paused on her

way to the kitchen to look in at her father. He was sleeping quietly, and though in the furtive morning light his face was but a thin, drawn shadow of its former full-fleshed ruddiness, it did hold a faint color and a slowly resurgent substance which gave weight to Doc Venable's opinion that the long haul to full recovery was finally under way. Which, she mused gravely, while sipping at a steaming cup, was cause for thankfulness. And would have been more so but for the presence in Reservation of that deputy sheriff, that Grady Haskell.

As always, when she thought directly of the man, a tinge of quickening color washed through her cheeks. For, so long as she lived, she doubted she'd ever forget the experience she'd gone through in his hotel room. The desperately impractical thinking which had set her to prowling the room in the first place, then her initial fright at being caught red-handed by the man himself. Finally, her even greater fright and shame and fury when his arms were about her and his lips a fiery, bruising force upon her own.

And something more, something stronger than all the first furious, anger based emotions. A breathlessness that had lingered, a quickening all through her, an awakening of feeling which had startled and dismayed her, and which she had set out to throughly stamp on and eradicate. And which persisted in spite of her.

Be-deviled to restlessness by her thoughts, she left the table and crossed to a window, through which she could observe both bunkhouse and cookshack. She was anxious for a talk with Sandy Lee. For Sandy had been in town last night and she wanted his report. Was Grady Haskell still in Reservation and if so, what was he about?

A man stepped from the cookshack. It was Vince

114

Tendler, pausing to lick an after-breakfast cigarette into shape. This done and alight and with the smoke of it curling back across his shoulder he came on toward the ranchhouse at his heavy, thrusting stride.

A frown puckered Katherine Levening's forehead. What was she going to do with this fellow, Vince Tendler? How was she to make him understand the extent of his authority and hold him in check to the limits of her own wishes and orders? This was another problem that had arisen to worry her.

She had known some liking for Vince. So far as she knew he was faithful to Hayfork and its interests. A tremendous worker, he drove himself without mercy and carried the crew along to like endeavor, while ruling them with an iron hand. All of which, at this particular time, was highly desirable.

Yet, balanced against these good points were several disturbing and irritating ones. Such as a growing, stubborn insistence that he alone knew best how to handle all ranch affairs, and the way of late he'd flatly ignored several of her plainly expressed wishes. It was as though he considered Hayfork his own and was out to run it so.

At the kitchen door he knocked briefly, then entered without waiting answer or summons. Which brought Katherine around in open displeasure.

"Vince, I wish you'd wait for me to answer your knock, instead of come pushing in this way. Anyone would get the impression you owned the place!"

He did not answer. He did not even seem to hear her. He was scowling over some problem of his own. He selected a cup from the wall cupboard, turned to the stove and poured himself coffee from the steaming pot. Still scowling, he began drinking it, black.

He made a burly, solid figure, standing there with his feet spread, his shirt open on his heavy chest, and stretched tight across his back and forward leaning shoulders. There was about him something bull-like, an obstinacy and ever challenging truculence. Gulping another swallow of coffee, he made a flat announcement.

"I'm going to fire Sandy Lee!"

She stared at him. "You're going to—what? Fire Sandy Lee? Indeed you'll do nothing of the kind! I can't imagine what ever gave you such a ridiculous idea, but it certainly is ridiculous. Sandy is the oldest, most faithful rider on this ranch. He's been with Hayfork as far back as I can remember. Dad would never leave him go and neither will I. So long as there is a Hayfork ranch, Sandy Lee will be part of it. That's final!"

"Nothing's final," said Tendler flatly. "And Jim Levening isn't running Hayfork now, or in condition to know what's best for it. Me, when I order a hand to do a thing, I expect it to be done. When it isn't, then that man is through, so far as I'm concerned. I don't care who he is or how long he's been with the outfit."

"What order did Sandy refuse to obey? I mean a legitimate one."

Tendler shrugged. "He's been a little uppish for some time, doing more what it pleases him to do, instead of what he's told. Just now in the cookshack I asked him what he'd heard and seen in town last night. He wouldn't tell me, saying he was going to report direct to you. He might as well told me it was none of my damn business."

"I don't think he meant it that way at all," Katherine defended. "It's just that he likes to talk things over with me. Sandy Lee helped raise me, and he's just like a second father to me."

Tendler shrugged again. "I don't know anything

116

about that. All I do know is he does what I tell him, or he's through on this ranch!"

Katherine moved to face him directly. She spoke sharply, for now she was sharply angry.

"Vince, it's time you and I had a real understanding! You are not making final judgement on all Hayfork affairs. I am! I am running Hayfork until my father is able to be up and around and able to take over again. You've begun to assume too much. You are foreman of this ranch, but nothing more than that. And should it come to a choice of whether you or Sandy Lee leaves the ranch, then it will be you who rides out. Is that thoroughly understood?"

Cup at his lips, Tendler peered narrowly at her past the rim of it, silent. She knew the frustrated feeling of having delivered an ultimatum to a rock wall, and with no more effect. Abruptly he tipped back his head, swallowing the rest of his coffee. He put the empty cup aside and pasted his cigarette in the corner of his mouth again, sucking deeply on it. Slowly he answered.

"Anybody would think I'd been making a lot of mistakes?"

"Not exactly. Though there was no sense behind the attack on that—that deputy, Grady Haskell. It was a brutal, stupid thing, which served no good purpose at all."

"How do you know it didn't?" Tendler retorted. "Another serving of such out of the same dish and he'll probably run for cover. He'll get out of these hills and stay out."

She studied him, marking the burliness of him, the arrogant manner in which he stood, feet spread, head and shoulders thrust forward as though ready to charge right over any obstacle that came in his path, the heat of a vast intolerance in his eyes. Like it or not, she admitted to herself, this man carried an impressive atmosphere of power about him, even though it was strictly a physical thing. He was the sort to beat his way to an objective by sheer brute strength and dogged brute persistence. Now he spoke again.

"Things you're forgetting, facts you're not looking at. You say you are going to boss Hayfork until your father is able to take over again. Well, it's hardly an even gamble Jim Levening will ever come back that far. Even if he should make it, it will be a damned long haul. So, while we consider that fact, let's consider this one.

"There's nothing Rutt Dubison and his Beaverhead crowd would like better than a chance to strip these hills of Hayfork cattle. Who's keeping them from it, right now? I am. Me—Vince Tendler! And doing it because I keep the crew tough and ready. Should I leave, in three months time you won't have a dozen head of cattle left. If I were you, I'd do a little thinking on that fact."

Anger still held her, but now also she knew a mounting uncertainty and unease. She and Vince had argued ranch issues before, but never had he been this blunt and defiant. The worst of it was—every word he said was true!

Doc Venable might be right or he might be wrong on her father's chances for eventual recovery. While Rutt Dubison and his wild Beaverhead crowd definitely had looked long and covetously at Hayfork range and cattle. Which was something her father had well known and guarded against, and which was in fact, fundamentally responsible for his present condition.

She made a weary little gesture.

"Oh, let's not quarrel, Vince. We've enough to worry about without that. You're right about our general situation and I know how valuable you are to us. I don't mean to interfere."

"Better," Tendler said. "Much better. And," he added, with a flat truculence, "I still say Sandy Lee does as I tell him or he gets paid off!"

Sounded another knock at the kitchen door and to Katherine's summons it was Sandy Lee himself who stepped in. He sensed the tension in the air immediately and his shrewd, puckered glance struck swiftly back and forth.

"Maybe I better step outside again?"

"No!" Katherine's exclamation was quick. "No, Sandy. Vince—I—we were waiting to hear from you. That deputy—he's still in town?"

"Still with us," Sandy nodded, with dry emphasis. "And something you can bet on—he'll be with us until he gets what he came into this country for. He won't be bluffed out, scared out or whipped out. Something Rutt Dubison and his crowd learned the hard way, last night."

"Rutt Dubison!" Vince Tendler was jarred into heavy query. "What about Rutt Dubison? You mean he and Haskell tangled?"

"That's what—plenty! And after the smoke cleared, Dubison and his brave lads snuck off home with their tails between their legs, minus all their guns, with Rudy Shedd dead across his saddle and Dubison with his face half bashed in by the butt of Joe Peele's old Greener shotgun. Yes, sir! I saw a tough man in action last night—a very tough man!"

Vince Tendler made a restless half turn.

"That don't add up. No one man handles Rutt Dubison and his crowd rough and single handed."

"This one man did," Sandy declared. "Grady Haskell did. I was there and I saw it. He handled them and made them like it."

119

"How—how did it happen, Sandy?" Katherine's interest was quick, just a shade breathless.

Sandy told it as he had seen it, softening no angle of it. Finishing, he wagged his grizzled head in reflective admiration.

"I say it again—that fellow Grady Haskell is all man. A fair one, too. He thanked me decent as you please for collecting the guns off that Beaverhead crowd."

"Which was a fool move on your part," accused Tendler. "It will set Dubison against Hayfork more than ever. It wasn't your place and you had no call to help Haskell."

"I had plenty of call," retorted Sandy. "First because Haskell told me to do it, and second because I was plumb tickled to see Dubison and his crowd well eared down. As for setting Dubison against Hayfork, he was always that, anyway. But it'll be considerable time before he'll feel like throwing rocks at us or anybody else. When he left town he was one sick hombre. His men had to lift him on his horse and then hold him there. No, from now on, Rutt Dubison don't scare me worth a damn. For I saw him cut down to size, last night—cut way down!"

"You," growled Tendler, "sound like you're glad to have this Haskell fellow hanging around. Maybe you're forgetting why he's here and what he can do to this ranch and the people on it?"

"I ain't forgetting a thing," Sandy defended. "But I am seeing clearer than I did. Katie girl, we been going at this all wrong. We can't keep covering up forever. Your friends in town, and Jim's, they been doing the best they know how, trying to help by blurring out the trail. But none of it's going to work. You can't fool this man Haskell, and you can't stop him."

"Maybe," said Tendler, heavily sarcastic, "you're suggesting we tell him everything? Would that be it?"

Sandy nodded soberly. "That's exactly it. One way or another, Haskell is going to dig up the truth about Jack Breedon. I feel we'd make our case a lot better if we quit trying to cover up and came out with the truth."

Vince Tendler turned to Katherine Levening.

"Well, there you have him. Your fine, life-long friend and faithful defender. The man neither you or Jim Levening would ever fire. And he'd sell you out to a snooping star packer!"

Sandy's reaction was instantaneous and explosive.

"That's a damn lie!"

Tendler wheeled, took a threatening step.

"You'd call me a liar? Why, you—!"

"Hold it!" broke in Sandy, coldly harsh. "Stay put, Tendler—stay right there! You throw a fist my way and I throw a gun on you—and use it! I'm too old a man to take a beating from such as you. Which reminds me of something. Haskell wanted to know if I'd had any part in ganging him his first night in town. I felt good being able to look him in the eye and say I didn't. For it's my hunch all who did will be damned sorry before he's done with them. Stack Coulter's already found out some about that. Others will, later."

"Go on," gritted Tendler, "go on! You're talking yourself right out of a job. Taking sides against your own outfit."

"Another lie," charged Sandy. "I been looking after Hayfork interests more years than you've been alive. Now what's this about me talking myself out of a job?"

"I told Kate I was going to fire you," Tendler said with obvious relish. "Now she knows why. She's heard it with her own ears."

121

Sandy pulled up, straight and quiet.

"That the way it's going to be, Katie girl? You're letting this bucko fire me?"

Katherine's answer was an impulsive little cry that came straight from her heart.

"Of course not! Not that—not that ever! Vince, I told you Sandy would never leave Hayfork."

Tendler faced her, burly, stolid, bull-stubborn. His words ran a little thick.

"And I told you what would happen if I did. Think it over—good!"

He turned to the door, went out and slammed it behind him.

Sandy pulled a chair up to the kitchen table, sat down in it, then put his quiet gaze on Katherine.

"Seems there's things I should know about, Katie. Tell me."

She sat down across from him and, leaning forward, elbows on the table top, pressed finger tips against her temples, her glance on emptiness.

"We argued some," she explained. "Probably I shouldn't have mentioned it at all."

"Mentioned what?" prompted Sandy.

"Well, for some time I've felt Vince was taking a lot for granted, almost as though he considered himself owner of Hayfork instead of just foreman. He's taken to walking right into this house without hardly bothering to knock. He did it this morning and it made me angry. So, when he began talking about firing you, I lit into him.

"I reminded him that he was just the foreman, not the owner of Hayfork. And I told him if it ever came to a choice of he or you leaving the ranch, he'd be the one riding out. To which he said he was the one keeping Rutt Dubison and the Beaverhead crowd away from Hayfork cattle, and claimed that if he ever left

122

Hayfork, Dubison would start raiding us. Which, I suppose, is true enough."

Her words ran out into a little silence. Then her head lifted and her eyes were misty.

"Oh, Sandy—why must arguments come at a time like this? We've enough to worry about without fighting among ourselves."

"Katie," said Sandy gently, "You're worrying unnecessary, and borrowing trouble that ain't here yet. First, like I said before, Rutt Dubison ain't going to be bothering anybody for quite some time. When he does, it won't be Hayfork he'll be looking at. He'll have a chore regaining the respect of the Beaverhead crowd so they'll follow him again. After that he'll be pointing at Grady Haskell. For if he don't even up with Haskell, then he'll lose out with the Beaverhead gang; they won't back him no more.

"Second, the only way you could get Vince Tendler to leave Hayfork, would be to run him off with a gun. You say he's acting like he owned the ranch. Well, that's exactly what he's figuring on—owning it. And the real reason he'd like to read my time is because he knows I got him figured and he's afraid I'll put a burr under his saddle."

Blinking back the mist of tears, she stared, wide-eyed.

"You say Vince expects to own Hayfork? How could he ever do that?"

"Simple enough, Katie. By marrying you."

"Marrying me? Sandy, that's not even funny!"

"No, it ain't," admitted the old rider. "But it's true, just the same. You mean you never figured him to have such an idea? Why, it's plain as day to me and others."

Flushing, she shook her head. "I never guessed. Nothing of the sort has ever occurred to me."

"Why not?"

"For several reasons. The principal one, probably, because I'm not in love with Vince Tendler in the slightest degree and never will be. And I certainly wouldn't think of marrying a man I did not love. Sandy, you're sure Vince is thinking so?"

"Y'betcha he is! Why shouldn't he? You're a mighty handsome girl, Katie. One of these days Hayfork will be all yours. The man you marry will take over. Vince Tendler figures to be that man. There you have it."

"But I'm not remotely interested right now in the idea of marriage. When and if I ever am, you may be sure of one thing. The man won't be Vince Tendler."

"Well now!" Sandy exclaimed heartily, "that sure sets my mind to rest on one point. Should I had to, I think I'd have done most anything to keep you from ever marrying such as Tendler. Any woman who ever married that man would be set for a lifetime of misery and unhappiness. Because Vince Tendler's wife would never be anything more to him than just another of his possessions."

Katherine was silent for a considerable time, her eyes big and dark with the turmoil of her thoughts. Presently she stirred.

"But he has been faithful and hard working for Hayfork. He deserves some credit for that."

"Now I wonder!" drawled Sandy cynically. "It could be you know, that he figures a day's work for Hayfork now, will add up to a day's work done for Vince Tendler, later on, when he owns the ranch. I'll lay you a bet, Katie. The day Vince Tendler gets it through his bull head, good and solid, that he ain't ever going to own Hayfork, that day his ambition in the ranch's affairs will die out quick. You wait and see."

Katherine pushed back from the table, got up and began moving restlessly about the room. She paused before the stove and poured another cup of coffee for herself and one for Sandy.

"That other thing you spoke of, Sandy—telling everything to that deputy. Do you really mean it?"

Sandy nodded vigorously.

"Sure I mean it. When you consider all that's happened since Grady Haskell arrived in Reservation, it's plain enough that he means business. One way or another, he's going to get his answers. We're trying to dodge the inevitable. So I say again it would be all to our advantage to give the plain truth to a man I'd bet is a square shooter and one who'll give us every break he can."

"If only Dad was well enough to understand and give his opinion!" Unable to stay still, Katherine circled the room again, feverish with tension and anxiety. "For it is his right to decide, and only his—not yours or mine, Sandy. I want to think on it. I got to be very sure. I'd never forgive myself if we did talk and it turned out wrong."

"Sure, Katie—sure," soothed Sandy. "We'll think on it."

10

WAITING OUT THE days until his letter to Bill Hoe could bring an answer, Grady Haskell moved leisurely about getting down to breakfast on still another morning, so again had the room to himself. Ruby Peele was waiting on table and, as she moved quickly back and forth clearing used gear away, Haskell watched her with quiet approval. She carried a bright, new mood, humming to herself as she went cheerfully about her work.

On the pretense of wanting more coffee, Haskell beckoned her over. He smiled and said:

"I like the looks of him, Ruby."

Startled, she stared. Ruby Peele had mixed feelings about this lean, deeply tanned, blunt featured man of the law. In a sort of scary, little girl way she liked him, but mainly her feeling was one not far from awe. For she knew the explosive ruthlessness which lay beneath the quiet, impassive exterior.

With her own eyes she had watched him savage down Stack Coulter. And she had heard over and over of how he had handled Rutt Dubison and the Beaverhead crowd in the Canyon House, night before last; a starkly brutal story of a man getting the life blasted out of him by a charge of buckshot at point blank range, and of another clubbed to senselessness with a crushing gun butt.

And it was this man sitting here, this man smiling

127

at her with a certain kindness in his crinkled eyes, who had done these things. At this moment it was a hard thing to believe. While the drawling remark just made puzzled her. She stammered a little.

"The looks of—of who?"

"Why, Neal Andrews, of course."

She colored furiously. Haskell's smile broadened.

"Yes, sir—I did like the looks of that boy. Just where is this cabin he's fixing up for the lady of his choice?"

"Up in—in Seneca Basin." With a burst of youthful pride she added, "He—Neal's got better than seventy head of cattle, too—all his own."

"Well now," approved Haskell, "that shapes up like a real fine start for a pair of young folks: a cabin and a herd, all clear."

Here was unexpected interest and understanding and she glowed under it. Shyly she went on.

"There's plenty of good water and a clear of ground for a garden, too. Neal said we—we'd—" she colored deeply again and came near stammering to a stop, then closed with a little rush, "have to skimp some at first."

"Nothing wrong with that," vowed Haskell. "I reckon skimping might be a heap of fun when there's two to share it. When are you and Neal going to face the preacher?"

Again she was self-conscious and squirming, yet breathlessly eager to share a confidence with someone who seemed to understand and was besides, honestly interested.

"Next—next spring, I guess. Neal, he wants everything to be as right and comfortable for me as possible."

"And you," Haskell said swiftly, "would be happy to share a leaky tent with him, wouldn't you?"

128

Abruptly this glowing, breathless, bright faced young girl stood as a woman grown. There was the swell of quiet pride in the way she straightened, and her glance, as she met Haskell's eyes, was serene and steady and all-wise.

"Yes," she said simply, "I would."

He applauded again. "Good girl! Now there is one more thing you must do."

"What is that?"

"Share the good news with your father."

She stiffened, and a hardness settled about her lips as she started to turn away. Haskell stopped her with a swift hand on her arm.

"A minute, youngster. Your father was a good man, once—and will be again. Have you ever thought of it that way?"

It seemed she was going to refuse an answer. Then her reply came, and coldly.

"I only know he's the town drunk."

"He was such, but no more," Haskell corrected. "He has a job now, working for Jim Kineen at the stable."

"I know," she said tonelessly. "A job which will last only until he gets his first pay. Then it will be the same old thing again."

"No. There you're wrong, Ruby. Joe Peele has already had an advance in wages, and not a dime gone for whiskey. Instead, all for a man's regained self-respect. I know how much it would mean to him if you'd go see him. There isn't anything he wouldn't do or give to have you respect him."

"Respect him!" she cried softly. "When did he ever give me cause for such? What concern did he ever have for my self-respect—with him the town drunk?"

"No matter," insisted Haskell. "What's past is past. Just because a person may have been in the wrong

129

once is no reason they must stay so forever. If your father was ever under a shadow, he's out in the clear open, now. Go see him. It will make him happy, and you, too."

She was studying him with a wondering light of appraisal in her clear young eyes. But there was adult wisdom in the question she put to him.

"Why—why should you care, either way? You've been here in Reservation less than a week. You can't know my father too well, and you hardly know me at all. So, why should you care?"

Haskell was silent while he lit a cigar. His face settled into grave lines and a sober brooding darkened his eyes. Slowly he nodded.

"A fair question deserving a fair answer. Why should I care? I'll tell you as best I can. Partly it is because I like your father and I like you. The rest, I think, has to do with the desire to square myself."

"Square yourself?"

"That's right." He got to his feet and stood looking down at her. His tone ran somber. "A couple of nights ago I killed a man. I had to, or be killed myself. From all I hear, he deserved killing. Which isn't the point. The point is—I killed him. When I pulled the trigger of that gun I watched everything go out of him. It took only an instant—a split second. Life and death were no further apart than that. And I wielded the power."

He paused and drew a deep inhale of smoke.

"Call it part of my job. Say that such things are needful at time when enforcing the law. I suppose they are. For that matter the man wasn't the first, for me. Chances are he won't be the last. In the face of necessity or the fury of a fight you don't stop to think about such things. You can't afford to. If you do, you're dead. Later, when it is over, when the smoke

130

clears away and the madness burns out, you think about it, plenty! And because you've taken away, you feel you should give in return. So you set out to scare up a little more happiness in life for someone. Which is about as close as I can come to explaining it."

There was no pull of hardness or bitterness about her lips now. Instead, they were soft and trembling a little. And her eyes were faintly misty.

"You're a very lonely man at times, aren't you?"

"At times," he admitted quietly. "Then I find another friend and the world's all right again."

She blinked rapidly and her words fell whisper soft. "I'll go see Pa."

In Jim Kineen's stable two old box stalls had to be torn out and new ones built. At this task Joe Peele toiled. It was a pleasuring, sweating labor. The measured whine of the saw biting through clear lumber, the hard rap-rap of a hammer driving home a nail, the keen, resin smell of fresh pine sawdust— these things were all to the good, telling as they did of a man building something needed and worth while. Though somewhat thinly and offkey, Joe Peele whistled his content.

The distant, mellow reasonance of the hotel dinner gong startled him. Noon already! Where had the hours gone? Putting aside his tools he scrubbed the sweat from his face and surveyed his morning's work with satisfaction. And decided that if he wasted no time getting a quick bite of lunch and then got right back to the job, he'd have one stall done by dark.

He went out the back way and over to the river, then along the bank of this to his cabin. Abruptly his head came up. A haze of smoke wreathed the tip of the cabin chimney and the good, suety fragrance of frying meat was in the air.

Now just who the devil—?

He wheeled around the corner of the cabin, stopped in the open doorway and went very still, staring with disbelief.

She turned from the stove, her greeting low and quiet.

"Hello, Pa."

Joe Peele finally found husky voice.

"Ruby—Ruby girl! How—what—?"

"Mrs. Wall said she could manage dinner at the hotel today by herself. I came over to cook you a good meal. I saw you coming, so put on the steak."

He scrubbed a hand across his eyes, as if still doubting the reality of what he saw. "You—this—." Again his words frittered out, his face working with emotion.

"Go wash up, Pa," she said gently. "The steak is near done."

He scrubbed in the clear, cold river water and it sharpened and steadied him. He came back into the cabin, toweling vigorously. With a broken comb he smoothed the scanty grayness of his hair.

She sat across the table from him, ate with him. Her touch around the old stove had a magic in it. Hot food, cooked for him by his own daughter! Never had he expected or dared hope for anything like this.

Wisely, she gave him a time of silence in which to get a grip on himself. Then:

"I heard you working. You're building something at the stable?"

"Yes. Fixing up some stalls. Ruby, girl—you don't know what this means to me."

She nodded. "I know. It means a lot to me, too."

He was all eagerness now.

"I'll fix up this old cabin. I'll build on a brand new room for you. I'll make up to you for all the years—."

She shook her head.

132

"Mrs. Wall needs me at the hotel most of the time, and I got a good room there. But I'll come see you as often as I can, and cook things for you. Which will be all right, won't it?"

All right? Why everything was all right now, and everything in him was humble.

"Whatever suits you best, child. And I'll yet make you proud of me."

Bright mistiness grew in her eyes as she looked at him.

"Sure you will, Pa. Now eat your dinner."

Good as each of these moments were, he could not drag them out. For soon she was brisk and busy at the dishpan.

"I'll clean up," she said across her shoulder. "You get on back to your work."

For a little time he still lingered, watching her, and she was wonderful in his eyes, strong and young and alert and beautiful. Ruby—his own girl! His! And if he had ever known a cry for the wasted years, it was far overshadowed by the deep thankfulness of this moment.

Her father gone, Ruby worked on in the cabin. She finished washing and drying the dishes, after which she busied herself shaking out the blankets of the bunk and making this up again, neatly. As she moved about she made mental note of things to be done in the future.

The stove and chimney needed a good cleaning and polishing, and some more shelves would be useful. Also, these would be lined with oil cloth, and a square of the same would cover the old table. Then, some kind of covering against the rough barrenness of the floor would help a lot. Maybe, she thought, Amos Potter would let her have that piece of old carpet that was rolled up and stored in a certain hotel back closet.

About to leave, she caught a whiff of drifting cigar smoke and stepped outside to find Grady Haskell sitting on the bench beside the door. He got to his feet, smiling.

"Well, was I right or wrong?"

Her answer was swift, breathless.

"So very right! We—Pa and I—owe you a great deal, Mr. Haskell."

"Not Mister, Ruby," he said. "Makes me feel too old. I'll answer to Grady."

She laughed gaily. "Very well—Grady." Then she added, laying a hand on her breast, "In here I am quiet, now. And very happy."

"Of course you are," nodded Haskell. "That is old man conscience at rest. And it squares me."

They went across the interval toward town, Ruby eagerly explaining her plans for her father's cabin.

Incoming hoofs rattled across the river bridge and two riders wheeled into town, one hauling up at the Canyon House, the other coming on to stop at Jellick's store. It was Vince Tendler who swaggered into the Canyon House, and Katherine Levening who made quick tie at the store hitch rail; then climbed the steps and crossed the porch to the wide, shadowed doorway. She was about to step through this when Grady Haskell and Ruby Peele moved into view past the corner of the store.

Haskell's head was inclined to one side and an easy, tolerant smile was on his lips as he listened to his companion's excited chatter. They angled on across street to the hotel, unaware of Katherine's presence. Frowning, she watched them, then, restless with a disturbing irritation, turned quickly into the store.

Milo Jellick came along behind the counter.

"Hello, Katie," he greeted. "If it's mail you're looking for, it isn't in yet. I don't know when Whit Hovey has been this late. He must have run into some sort of trouble along the way." Dropping his voice somewhat, he asked, "How is Jim doing?"

"Better each day," she answered. "I have real hope now that Doctor Venable is right about father's chances."

Despite the confident way she said this, there was a shadow of listlessness in her tone and manner that made Milo Jellick study her shrewdly.

"You're worrying too much, Katie," he observed kindly. "You've done all you could. The rest of us have done all we could. Now it is up to the fates."

"And now," she said, "Sandy Lee thinks we'd have been smarter if we'd admitted everything to Grady Haskell, right from the first."

Jellick pursed his lips, bobbing his head slowly up and down. "Jim Kineen says the same. He and Sandy could be right. What does Vince Tendler think?"

"Just the opposite. And that another man-handling would run Haskell out of the country."

"He's dead wrong, there," Jellick exclaimed with quick decisiveness. "This fellow Haskell has definitely shown he's not the running sort. You heard about his tangle with Rutt Dubison and the Beaverhead crowd?"

She nodded. "Sandy Lee heard it all, saw it all. One—one man was killed?"

"And lucky there wasn't more. Would have been if Dubison and the others hadn't knuckled under, quick and complete. This man Grady Haskell is a little difficult to figure. In some ways he's thoroughly kind and considerate. But in a fight he can be a ruthless savage. You'd better make Vince Tendler understand that, Katie."

She tipped her shoulders in a faint shrug. "I'm afraid Vince has reached the point where I can't tell him anything, any more."

"So-o!" Jellick murmured. "It's begun to show openly, has it?"

"You mean his trying to run everything?"

"That's it, Katie. Jim Kineen and me, we've long figured that the desire was there, sort of, well—germinating, shall we say? And, Vince being the arrogant, opinionated sort that he is, it was bound to come into the open, sooner or later. You've rowed with him about it?"

"Some. Now there is a sort of uneasy truce. Vince rode into town with me."

Outside sounded the grind of wheels, the rattle of trace. Milo Jellick, head turned as he listened, nodded his satisfaction.

"There's the stage now. We'll soon have a look at that mail."

He hurried out, the stage just pulling to a halt at the edge of the porch. The driver, a dried up, whiskery little gnome of a man, tossed down the mail sack.

"Long time since you've been this late, Whit," said Jellick.

"Long time since I had a horse pick up a stone bruise," Whit Hovey retorted. "My off leader did, crossing Big Pine Wash. Best horse in the team, too, and I wasn't taking no chances of laming it permanent. So, I came in from Big Pine at a walk."

The stage creaked away, stableward, the off leader limping badly.

Milo Jellick carried the mail sack inside, emptied it on the counter and began sorting through the contents. At the door, Grady Haskell showed, pausing there a moment as he glimpsed Katherine Levening.

Then he came ahead, his hand lifting to the brim of his hat. He did not speak, just stood waiting, his glance shifting to Milo Jellick.

The first piece of mail Jellick had selected from the little pile on the counter, was a well-stuffed, legal sized envelope. After glancing at the address, he held it out to Haskell.

"What you've been waiting for. By the size and weight, Bill Hoe must have had a lot to get off his mind."

"Would seem so," nodded Haskell laconically.

He carried the envelope back to his hotel room before opening it. It held a brief note and half a dozen copies each of two different reward dodgers, so lately from the press they smelled strongly of printer's ink. One of these put five hundred dollars on the head of Frank Gentile. The other offered a thousand dollars for information leading to the locating of Deputy Sheriff Jack Breedon.

The note was brief and to the point:

Use these dodgers wherever they'll do the most good. The County Commissioners have approved both the money and the purpose. Good luck!
William J. Hoe.

Haskell pocketed one each of the dodgers, put the rest in his saddlebags, then returned to the store. Katherine Levening was still there, talking with Milo Jellick. Their conversation stopped pointedly as he appeared. Rather obviously, they had been discussing him. They watched him in silence as he came up to the counter.

"Some tacks," he said. "And the loan of a hammer."

Milo Jellick straightened.

"Why would you want such?"

"To put a couple of reward dodgers up, outside."

"Not on my building!" objected the storekeeper, quickly and with vehemence.

Haskell's face hardened. "Jellick," he demanded curtly, "when are you going to quit playing the altruistic fool? This is law business. When are you going to understand that? Law business! Not you, or anyone else in this town or in these hills is going to stop it. There are answers hereabouts that the law wants. And one way or another, it's going to find them. Now I'll take the hammer and the tacks!"

Milo Jellick hesitated, trying to hold Haskell's boring glance, and failing. He shrugged and produced the requested articles. Simmering a little, Haskell stepped outside, turned left and fastened the dodgers to the store front, side by side. As he finished, there was the scuff of spur chains behind him and he came around to face Vince Tendler just climbing the porch steps. Also, Katherine Levening now stood in the doorway, her eyes big and dark with some kind of torment of inner feeling.

Vince Tendler crossed the porch with his heavy swagger. His broad cheeks carried a faint whiskey flush and his eyes were the usual heated pits of an arrogant intolerance.

Facing Tendler, Grady Haskell knew a surge of primitive feeling yeasting up inside him. There was a violent something between him and this man Vince Tendler. It had raised its head the first moment they met, back on Rancheria Creek at the time of the wolf killing incident. It was here, now. And it would always be present between them, no matter the time or the place.

For the overbearing push of challenge in Tendler's manner was bound to strike up swift answering reac-

138

tion in any strong willed, prideful man. It was a thing which made for instinctive hatred, relentless and bitter. And it was a thing which Grady Haskell knew now.

In addition he owned a harsh memory. And bruises, scarce healed. For it was Vince Tendler who had led the pack that manhandled him, his first night in Reservation. So there too, was a score to be evened. For the moment, however, mindful of other things, Haskell was willing to let such reckoning wait another time. Just now it was more important that he observe some reactions and analyze them, and so perhaps gain further lead toward the answers he was seeking. Stepping past Katherine Levening in the doorway, he returned hammer and box of tacks to Milo Jellick's counter. After which he sauntered outside again.

Both Katherine Levening and Vince Tendler stood reading the dodgers. With an abrupt, growling curse, Tendler ripped down the one concerning Jack Breedon, crumpling it in his fist.

Haskell's words hit tersely. "That was a mistake, Tendler. You tore it off, now you put it back!"

Tendler came around, mouth pulled to a thin mockery. "Like hell I will!"

He was flouting the star and its authority as baldly as Rutt Dubison had done.

Dangerously soft, Haskell said: "Like hell you won't!"

Speaking, he prowled forward.

Vince Tendler laughed and threw the crumpled dodger in Haskell's face.

From the doorway of the store, where he'd come up to watch, Milo Jellick let go a quick, breaking sigh.

"That does it!" he murmured.

11

IT WAS THE crumpled dodger, thrown so contemptuously in his face, that set Grady Haskell off, bleakly raging. On a few occasions in the past, stung to a similar gust of swift, blind fury, he had given way to equally swift, blind physical reaction, and always with near disaster as a result. It was so now, for Vince Tendler, watchful and calculating, ducked under the driving fist Haskell threw, and in return smashed him savagely under the heart, a lifting, powerful blow.

To Haskell it was as though paralysis had struck. Strength ran out of him, and how he managed to keep his feet, he never knew. Nor could he breathe, while the need for breath was an instant and frantic need in his aching lungs. Yet the blow, disabling as it was for the moment, had one aidful effect. It knocked all the blind, unheeding rage fog out of him, leaving a core of relentless purpose along with the desperate need of clear thought and cunning.

For Vince Tendler was coming at him, stalking him, fists knotted and ready, thick wrists hooked menacingly. This time it was at his head that a fist came, and only by the most desperate stretch of will was he able to avoid it. Missing, and following the blow with his forward driving weight, Tendler was off balance just long enough for Haskell to grab hold, which was the thing he knew he had to do; to grab, hang on, and wait for the numbing effects of that first deadly blow to lift.

Recovering his balance, Vince Tendler tried to pull clear, to earn enough distance in which to smash home another punch. But Haskell hung on tenaciously, and when Tendler tried to drive a fist into his face and knock him away, he ducked his head low against Tendler's chest and so thwarted the move. Tendler's next try to get clear was by rushing Haskell against the store front, slamming him into it viciously.

Head still bowed well forward, Haskell took the impact across the broad of his back and shoulders, so, while it shook him up, it did no real hurt. Contrariwise, it loosed all the numbed, locked up tensions in him. Now, of a sudden, he could breathe again, and as precious air rushed in and out of his laboring lungs, strength and coordination began to return.

Still fighting to tear away, Tendler hauled him out to the edge of the porch, then rushed him savagely across it to smash into the store front a second time, setting up a rumble of echoes through the building. Again Haskell took the impact across back and shoulders, and hung on, waiting things out a little longer.

Snarling, Tendler worried him back and forth. He was bull-strong, Vince Tendler was, supremely confident in this sort of business, and with crushing power in his heavy fists when he had room to swing from far back. But from close in he did not have too much drive behind his blows.

Abruptly Haskell braced his legs, stiffened his back and threw Tendler away from him. This was something Tendler had not expected, and the surprise of it caught him off guard. Before he could react, Haskell landed his first blow, hitting him in the mouth, solid and jarring, pulping Tendler's lips against his teeth, bringing a spurt of crimson.

Haskell moved as though to follow up, and Tendler tried to repeat his first maneuver of dodging low and driving another crusher to the body. But this time Haskell's move was a feint, and after suggesting it, he stepped back, letting Tendler's fist flail empty air. Then as Tendler, off balance, lunged by, Haskell clubbed him savagely across the back of the neck.

The power of this, plus the impetus of his own useless lunge, sent Vince Tendler floundering down to his hands and knees, the butt of his gun flaring wide past his hunched back and bent hips. Haskell grabbed the weapon, jerked it free and threw it out in the street. Then he set himself, and as Tendler came back to his feet, furiously turning, fists hooked and ready, Haskell blasted him solidly on the angle of his heavy jaw. Tendler went down again, rocked back on his haunches.

For ten long, ticking seconds he stayed that way, dazed and blinking, a vast unbelief on his face, the look of one unable to understand how such a thing could happen. He shook his head and came up, no longer full of headlong, heedless confidence, but with a calculating caution now, which made him doubly dangerous.

Katherine Levening had retreated to the doorway at the start of this thing, and she stood there now beside Milo Jellick, pale of face and strained of eye. Once she called out.

"Stop it, Vince—stop it! There's no sense—!"

"No use, you mean, Katie," broke in Milo Jellick, gripping her arm as though to hold her in safety. "This is something that must go to a finish!"

Neither Haskell or Tendler heard a word that the girl or Jellick said. Nor were they aware of their presence, nor did they see Jim Kineen and Joe Peele and Whit Hovey, the stage driver, come hurrying along the street from the stable. Or Art Oren step out of the Canyon House and Amos Potter from the hotel. Others appeared here and there, closing in on the store. It was the old, primal fever of a fight, the heat of stark hate and destroying fury between two men like a spreading odor to reach others and summon them to the source.

Fully committed by this time, Haskell and Tendler were intent only on each other. They weaved in and out along the porch, feinting back and forth, circling, waiting, watching for the one big chance with a deadly intensity. Already their exertions and concentrated purpose had them panting, mouths open, and from Vince Tendler's mashed lips little bubbles of crimson formed and blew outward.

In the end it was Tendler's intolerant arrogance and conceit which set off the next explosion of violent action. He had been knocked down by this man Grady Haskell, and the knowledge was the bitterest of gall and wormwood to him. So, despite a certain degree of caution, he was unable to match the icy, calculating patience which had descended on Grady Haskell. With a heavy throated growl, feral as that of a bear, Tendler drove in.

Awaiting just such a move, Haskell aimed another punch for the jaw angle, but it landed too far back, on the side of Tendler's neck. In return, Tendler's fist rammed into the middle of Haskell's chest. There was no particular effect either way from these two blows, for they were surface punishment, and both men were now immune to such. They were like wounded animals, so numbed by a first bullet as to be virtually impervious to the effect of another unless it be direct to some vital center.

So now they stood toe to toe and beat each other about the body and head and face until, as though by mutual understanding and agreement they stepped back to collect their forces and their breath for the next clash. Slowly they circled and circled. Tendler's spur chains dragging, Haskell's boot heels striking solid and measured on the planks of the porch. Both were bleeding at the mouth now; both had lifting, darkening welts about the face. Haskell cleared his throat and spat, then gave out with uneven words.

"You'll put—that dodger back—or I'll—whip you until—you do—!"

Tendler's answer was a mumbled curse and another headlong charge. And Haskell, aiming for the jaw angle again, found it squarely with a rifling smash that knocked Tendler flat. Catching Tendler coming in, adding the weight of his rush to the power of it, it was by far the most damaging blow of the fight. It hurt Tendler badly, and he lay as he was for a long moment, blinking stupidly. Then, as he rolled over and crawled up to one unsteady knee, behind the stupidity a crimson glint of cunning showed, and he whipped a hand to his holster and found it empty.

"No use, bucko!" jeered Haskell thickly. "I took care of your gun some time back. For I knew—there was a streak I'd uncover—if I just kept digging. You—widestepping boys—are all alike. The big front is—to cover it up. The streak—I mean."

He moved in, merciless. Tendler lurched upright, tried to back away, but the effects of the knockdown made him slow and unsure. Haskell cornered him against the building and hit him three times, a right, a left, then another crashing right, all to the face. Tendler's knees shook and he slid down a little way. He tried to lunge into the clear, both arms wildly swinging. Haskell stepped inside them and gave Tendler back his first blow, a lifting hook under the heart.

Something not far from a groan erupted from Tend-

145

ler's throat. His mouth opened wide, his chin dropped, and a slime of crimson ran across it. His eyes turned dull and his head wobbled on his shoulders.

"Going to put—that dodger back?" demanded Haskell remorselessly.

Tendler tried a weakly pawing swing, which Haskell caught on a hunched left shoulder, and with a short, crossing right, dropped Tendler again, and Tendler lay there, openly sick and groaning now.

Vince Tendler had known his share of rough and tumble. He'd whipped more than his share of men, some of whom had been good with their fists. He'd been hit hard before, but never as he had this day. That lean, prowling man now standing over him, was all whale bone and rawhide, with fists that landed like chunks of thrown lead, to hurt a man clear down to his vitals.

Haskell turned away for a moment, his sweat fogged eyes searching. The crumpled reward dodger lay over against the wall, close to the door. Slowly he trudged to it, bent and picked it up, a drip of crimson from his lips falling to stain it. At this moment he was hardly a yard from Katherine Levening, and she was watching his every move with a horrified fascination.

On his part, Grady Haskell saw nothing save the adamant purpose which consumed him. With battered, clumsy hands he smoothed the dodger, then returned to where Vince Tendler had once more staggered erect, leaning against the wall for support. Haskell held the dodger out to him.

"Put it back!"

Tendler tried to slap it out of his hand.

Haskell hit him, dropping him once again.

"Put it back! I'll whip you until you do!"

Tendler lay still, making little moaning sounds.

146

Haskell collared him, hauled him erect, squared him around and dropped him with anther hooking punch.

"Put—it—back!"

Katherine Levening began to weep softly, Milo Jellick to mumble protest. He even took a short step in Haskell's direction as though he would interfere, but stopped as Jim Kineen's voice struck at him from the edge of the porch.

"Stay out of it, Milo! This is a lesson for Vince Tendler—a lesson for all of us. Stay out of it!"

Looking down at his man, Haskell droned:

"Put it back!"

Through the beating thunder and deathly gray sickness of his world, Vince Tendler finally realized there was no other answer but to obey. He felt blindly around for the dodger, got hold of it. It took him three lurching tries to get to his feet and stumble to the wall of the building. Here he made an effort to spread the dodger, too blind to see that he had it upside down. Twice he hit at it with his fist, clumsily, as though he would thus nail it to the wall. Then, with a shuddering half-sigh, half-moan, he crumpled down in a senseless heap.

Again Jim Kineen's voice struck across the waiting quiet.

"He tried, friend Haskell. You won your point. He was blind and out on his feet—but he tried!"

Slowly, tiredly, Haskell nodded.

"Yeah, I guess so. He made the gesture—he tried."

He picked up the battered dodger, where it had fluttered from Tendler's unconscious fingers. It was torn along one edge, badly wrinkled, and stained with the blood of both men. But it still said all it had said before, and legibly. He turned to Milo Jellick.

"Seems I'll need that hammer and tacks again."

Without a word of argument, Jellick fetched them,

and Haskell, stepping around the piled up figure of Vince Tendler, replaced the Jack Breedon reward notice to its original spot on the wall. This done, he made slow survey of the silent watchers and spoke with a flat emphasis.

"I guess everybody understands now that these things must stay where I post them!"

His direct glance settled on Katherine Levening.

"I'm sorry you had to see it. And there's no need weeping over Tendler. He'll live. His kind don't kill easy; they're just a little slow to learn."

She faced him with some defiance, but also with a baffled wonder, for, while a moment ago he was a man without mercy, savagely intent on beating another man into a state of complete subjugation, he now stood quiet and remote; a somewhat somber figure, peculiarly alone despite those grouped around.

"Did—did you have to treat him so?" she cried. "To make him crawl like—like a whipped dog? Did you have to do that?"

"I said he was slow to learn. The lesson was just as rough as I had to make it."

"But his pride!" she cried again. "When you trample a man's pride like that, you can kill some part of him—!"

"How about mine?" retorted Haskell. "I happen to know pride, too. Nor do I carry this—" he tapped the star on his shirt—"to stand still while its authority is being flouted and scorned by such as Vince Tendler. Also, I'm human enough to resent being ganged and kicked around by some self-appointed bucko boy and his friends. If Tendler's pride is so damn precious, let him show some consideration for that of others."

He strode along the porch, dropped off the end of it and headed for the hotel. He walked straighter than he felt, for he'd left a lot of energy back on the store

148

porch. Old bruises about his head and face had been beaten to a fresh soreness, and about his midriff, where Vince Tendler's best blows had landed, the nerve ends were all afire and crawling.

He was still yards short of the hotel when Ruby Peele came running to meet him. She had watched the fight from the hotel doorway, and for the second time had seen Grady Haskell whip a man down to a sprawled heap. All the awe she had felt toward him before was now returned, and she was wide eyed and stammering as she caught at his arm.

"Just so—you're all right—all right! Just so you're not hurt—too bad—!"

Her concern was so sincere and ingenuous, Haskell had to smile, despite physical misery and the deepening gloom of mental reaction.

"Not too bad," he assured her. "That fellow was like a mad bull, and wherever he hit, he left a mark. But I'll do all right."

She followed him to his room and made him lie down. She soaked towels in cold water and spread them in wet compress across his battered face. The result was soothing and restful and it wrung tribute from him.

"You're all right, youngster," he mumbled through muffling folds. "The pure quill."

Back at the store, his senses returning, Vince Tendler was up on one knee. But when Milo Jellick would have offered a hand to aid him to his feet, Tendler struck it aside with a violence that came near upsetting him again. His mouth hung half open and his eyes, though staring straight ahead, dull with shock, smoldered like partly covered coals. He put a spread hand against the store front and with this braced support pulled slowly upright.

He turned, dropping his shoulders against the wall,

staying so on spread feet while he mopped clumsily at his mouth and face with a scrubbing forearm. Slowly the shock faded from his eyes, the fire in them burning deeper and hotter.

"Vince," Katherine Levening said, choked and hesitant. "Vince——!"

If he heard her at all, he gave no sign, instead lurching to the porch steps then down these and along to where his horse stood tethered in front of the Canyon House. He loosed the tie of the reins, then stood for a little time as though gathering strength to mount.

When he did try, it took him two attempts before he made it into the saddle. Once up, however, he hauled his horse around with a sudden rip of reins and used the spurs so savagely the stung animal squealed its protest as it fled wildly out of town, its rider weaving from side to side.

Of those who had watched it all, Jim Kineen was the first to cross the porch and read the posted rewards. After which he came along to where Katherine Levening and Milo Jellick stood and spoke to Katherine with a grave kindliness.

"I'd have a word with you, Katie girl."

She nodded, turning back through the doorway. Milo Jellick moved to have his look at the notices, along with the rest of the curious ones. Inside the store, Jim Kinnen was somberly thoughtful as he got out his pipe, packed and lighted it. Katherine broke into this small interval of silence.

"I know what you're going to say; that the truth be given to Grady Haskell?"

"That's it," Kineen said. "I've told Milo Jellick as much."

Katherine nodded. "I know. Sandy Lee thinks the same. I——I wonder if you're right?"

"I'm sure of it," Kineen declared. He added words

150

almost identical to those Sandy Lee had spoken. "Haskell will not be stopped. One way or another he will find what he came for. So it would be far better that he hear the story from you than from some informer. For you would be telling the simple truth, while some one else, intent on that reward, might not be too careful with such."

Katherine hit her hands together. "If only the responsibility wasn't all mine!" she cried softly. "If only Dad were well enough to have his own voice in the matters!"

"Now I can understand your feelings there," Kineen sympathized. "But it never helps matters to put off a decision that must be made."

She took a small, restless turn, back and forth a few steps.

"When do you think I should see him?"

"Now!" Kineen said bluntly. "Nothing's to be gained, Katie, by waiting. The quicker matters are brought to a head, the quicker you'll know just where you stand, and so rid yourself of a lot of useless worry. If I were you, I'd take the truth to Grady Haskell this minute."

She turned, silent as she looked across the store's muted gloom at the bright rectangle of the doorway and the sunlit street beyond. She struck her hands together again, this time in a gesture of decision.

"Very well. I will go—now!"

She moved quickly into the street and crossed to the hotel. Here, as she stepped through the door, Ruby Peele came dropping down the inner stairs.

Katherine had known this girl for a long time, though never to the extent of any real feminine camaraderie or friendship, mainly because to her, Ruby had always seemed pretty much of a child. But when, a little bit ago, Ruby came running to meet Grady

Haskell out in the street, and claim his arm so fervently, realization struck that Ruby Peele was no longer a child, but instead a budding young woman, and a pretty one. And acceptance of this fact had brought with it to Katherine Levening, a shadow of swift, strange resentment.

Now she regarded Ruby for a silent moment before speaking.

"I'm looking for Mr. Haskell. Would he be in his room?"

"He is," came the faintly defiant, faintly hostile answer. "I've been caring for him. I don't believe he wants to see anyone else right now."

"I'll take a chance on that," Katherine retorted quietly, pushing past and climbing the stairs.

The door of his room was open. She paused, looking at the long length of him stretched out on the bed, a towel compress across his face. She remembered the last time she had been in this room, and the warmth of a quick flush beat through her cheeks. She moved across the threshold and, quiet as she was, he caught the rustle of movement, and his words came, muffled.

"Didn't take you long to get that fresh water, youngster."

Katherine drew a deep breath. "This is Katherine Levening."

He surged upright, whipped the towel off his face. His hair, water dampened, was tousled and awry, and past the bruises and the swellings, he stared at her with a startled, almost boyish wonder. Then, as he swung his feet to the floor and stood up, he was again a grave, reserved man.

"I don't quite understand," he said. "Why would you be here? There was something you wanted?"

Her courage nearly failed her. What she was about

to say would cast the die, irrevocably. She tried putting the moment off a little longer.

"I—I'm glad to see you weren't hurt too badly."

"Thanks for the concern," he said drily. "But that wasn't what you came here to say." He was watching her very steadily. "There was something else, wasn't there?"

Her head came up. "Yes. Something else. That reward notice which Vince Tendler tore down—you won't need it any longer. I can tell you about the man you're looking for."

"You mean—Jack Breedon?"

She nodded.

"I've the feeling," Haskell said slowly, "that Breedon could be dead. Am I right?"

She nodded again. "Yes, you're right."

"It was violent death?"

"Yes. He was shot."

"Would you know who killed him?"

"Yes." She had gone slightly pale, but her glance did not waver. "Yes, I know. My father did."

If she thought this statement would startle Haskell, she was wrong. For he nodded, soberly thoughtful.

"I had figured something of the sort. It had to be about like that. Where will I find your father, now?"

"At home," she said. "You need have no worry of him being a fugitive. It is no more than an even chance he'll ever walk or ride again."

Haskell waited, saying nothing. Presently she went on, her words subdued and toneless.

"In the fight, Dad was hit, too, and at first it seemed he must surely die. Doctor Venable managed to remove the bullet, which had lodged against the spine. For months it seemed certain Dad would be paralyzed, even if he did live, though Doctor Venable claimed steadily there was a chance for recovery. Yet at best, it will be months before he'll be able to leave his bed."

"Why do you come to me now?" Haskell asked. "Why not before?"

"I was not sure of the right," she answered. "It—it was bad enough to see my father in the condition he is, without setting the law after him, too."

"Yet, finally, you do just that. Why?"

"It has become increasingly plain you were bound to find out." With deep honesty she added, "It was not my thought entirely. Mainly I'm here because Sandy Lee and Jim Kineen both felt I should tell you. I'm sure Milo Jellick felt so, too."

She was a proud girl. Watching her closely, Haskell saw that this was costing her a great deal. He kept his words and manner quiet and mild.

"You speak of a fight taking place. I will have to know all about that."

"Of course," she agreed. "But not from me, because my word would be second hand. You must hear it from Sandy Lee, as he saw it. So, if you would ride out to Hayfork tomorrow morning—?"

Haskell nodded. "I'll be there." He showed the ghost of a dry smile. "I hope there won't be rifle bullets in the road ahead of me this time."

She flushed. "That wasn't a very smart thing for us to do, I admit. Afterwards, Sandy Lee said he felt like a fool."

"Good man, Sandy Lee," declared Haskell. "I like him. And you know, Katie Levening, your father must be a mighty good one, too."

She was moving toward the door, but now she stopped and came swiftly around. "What do you mean? Why do you say that?"

"Because of his many sincere friends. I've asked a lot of questions around this town, which, had they

154

been answered, I now see would have led me straight to him. But I got no answers; I got no place at all. And to have friends willing to cover up for him that way, a man has to be one that others like and respect deeply. I look forward to meeting him tomorrow."

Gravely she held Haskell's eyes, and now he saw a perceptible lessening of the tension in her, saw a softening grow about her lips, relaxing them to a sober sweetness.

"You will see a man gravely stricken," she said. "And you are being kinder to us than we have been to you, Grady Haskell. I thank you for that."

Now she left, and hurriedly, as though afraid of being somehow betrayed by this gentler mood. At the head of the stairs she met Ruby Peele returning with a pitcher of fresh water. The impulsive words which swept across Katherine Levening's lips, startled her as much as they did Ruby.

"Thank you, my dear, for caring for him!"

12

FROM THE DAY, months previous, when her father had come home across his saddle, Katherine Levening had been living with two great fears. The first was for her father's life, the second of the certain reckoning to come, even if he should recover. Because, in the fight that had left him so close to death, he had killed a man named Breedon, one who had carried a deputy sheriff's star into these Trinity Hills. Most certainly, she had known, the law would follow up and investigate Breedon's disappearance.

The investigation had appeared in the person of Grady Haskell, and it had become increasingly apparent there was no way of stopping the man; both he and his purpose were remorseless and certain. So, on the advice of shrewd and proven friends, she had now gone to him with the truth, and had found that not only was the telling a source of great relief, but the manner in which Haskell received it had left her feeling there was not so much to fear of the law, after all; that perhaps it could be considerate and just and benevolent.

In any event, as she made it now, she was finding the ride home much more pleasant than it had been coming to town. Momentous as the afternoon had been, what with the brutal physical showdown between Grady Haskell and Vince Tendler, her frame of mind was better than it had been for months. A great weight had lifted from her shoulders, a nagging mental pressure removed.

She thought of the man she had but recently faced in that upstairs hotel room, and her eyes grew big and dark as she recalled the way he beat Vince Tendler to a broken, cowed obedience. There were the words she had thrown at him concerning a man's pride, and the answer he had given. And the weary somberness of his mood as he tramped off to the hotel. There was more, like the way Ruby Peele had come running to meet him, with open anxiety and relief, and the disturbingly proprietary manner in which she had taken his arm to aid him. And afterward, in the hotel, that same manner, plus a challenging defiance.

Katherine straightened in her saddle, swung her shoulders restlessly. What business of hers what Ruby Peele said or how she felt toward Grady Haskell, or he toward her? For this man was the law, and could very well be the one to put her father behind bars. Or on a gallows . . . Then why had she said what she did to Ruby Peele as they passed on the stairs, thanking the girl for caring for Haskell? Where was her common sense?

Guiltily, she tried to put her thoughts elsewhere. On Vince Tendler. Here was one who deserved them. Here was one who had ridden at her right hand in the interests of Hayfork. Yet she'd been wasting her concern on the man who had whipped him so tragically. What on earth was the matter with her, anyhow?

She was still engrossed in this tangle of mental turmoil, when, through the long, smoky afternoon shadows of the timber it was Sandy Lee who came spurring to meet her. He swung to a stop beside her and she marked the grimness of him.

"Sandy! What is it? Not—not Dad?"

He shook his head.

"Nothing about your father. It's Tendler. He showed at the ranch, all beat to hell. It must have been Haskell who gave him the mauling, for now he's trying to get the crew to head back to town with him and get Haskell, once and for good. So far, only Stack Coulter and Dutch Orrock seem to be listening. Given time though, he might talk the others into it. And Katie, this outfit can't afford to fight with the law or dodge it any longer. If we try it we're only storing up more trouble for Jim Levening."

"I know," Katherine cried. "I know! I'll put a stop to that nonsense Vince is preaching."

"He's wild—he's crazy," Sandy warned. "I doubt he'll listen to you."

"Maybe he won't, but the others will. Come on!"

"That damned Tendler!" said Sandy bitterly.

She had been riding at a jog. Now she put her horse to a driving run, and by the time she and Sandy reached the home meadow, raced the length of it and up the incline to headquarters, both of their mounts were foaming.

Several of the crew were gathered about the bunkhouse door, and they shifted uneasily as Katherine and Sandy stormed in. Katherine was out of her saddle before her horse came to a full stop.

"Where," she demanded, "is Vince Tendler?"

A rider inclined his head. "Inside."

They made way for her and she moved toward the bunkhouse door. Before she could reach it, Vince Tendler stood in it. His appearance startled her, shocked her. Something had happened to this man besides a physical beating. More than the mere bruising residue of physical blows had coarsened his face. It was as though such blows had knocked aside a sur-

159

face covering, to uncover a primitive brutishness which had lain hidden just underneath.

This man had let go all hold of something which had once held him to a reasonable responsibility and respect. Observing him, she knew a shading of fear. For Vince Tendler was now aeons of time distant, far back in a swamp of savagery where she could never hope to reach him. Yet she tried.

"Vince, there will be no more talk of going to town and starting further trouble. I just came from having a talk with Grady Haskell. I told him the whole truth about Dad and his fight with Breedon. So we are now through quarreling with the law or trying to evade it. Understand—through!"

He stared at her without expression, his eyes sultry coals, small and remote behind hooded lids. When words finally came they fell gutturally thick across his puffed and battered lips.

"You got nothin' to say about it!"

"I have everything to say!" she retorted sharply. "Which is this. Any one of you who goes against my wishes in this matter, is no longer riding for Hayfork. Is that understood?"

She swung about, her glance touching different members of the crew. One of them, Jeff Keough, nodded. A solid, dependable sort, he was one whose opinion counted with the others.

"What's good enough for you, Miss Katie, is good enough for me. If you say you got nothing against this man Haskell and what he represents, then I sure ain't. Chores to do, you fellers. Let's get at 'em!"

He took the rein of Katherine's horse and moved away to the corrals. The others followed, scattering quickly as though anxious to get beyond the reach of Vince Tendler's gaze and voice. Dutch Orrock went with the rest, leaving only Tendler with Stack Coulter behind him in the bunkhouse, and Sandy Lee standing quiet but alert beside Katherine.

"You see, Vince," she said. "The rest understand. Now you must."

He spat on the earth.

"Hell with them! Coulter and me, we'll take care of Mister Deputy Sheriff Haskell. And right!"

"No! You heard what I said, Vince. Anyone who goes against my wishes in this, no longer rides for Hayfork. I mean that!"

Tendler spat again.

"Then I'm through. Any damn outfit that won't stand by its own, ain't worth riding for. I told you what would happen the day I was through. That day Hayfork starts coming apart. May take a little time, but that's how it will be. Something you can look forward to." He turned back into the shadows of the bunkhouse. "Roll your gear, Stack. We're riding out!"

Impulse to argue further with Vince, to try and reach him with reason and make him understand, started Katharine toward the bunkhouse step. But Sandy Lee caught her arm and drew her away.

"No! Let be what must be. You're the boss of this ranch, Katie. Make it stick. You start softening toward Tendler now, we'll be worse off than ever. Let him go. There's a man who's turned bad, and he'll never be any use again to this ranch or any other. We're better off without him."

"But—but he and Coulter will go to town after Grady Haskell. They'll start more trouble."

"Maybe they will," said Sandy drily. "Then again, maybe they won't. Remember, both of them took a going over from Haskell. They may hate him, but deep down inside they're remembering their lickings, and they won't be too anxious for more of the same. You notice Tendler wanted the whole crew to ride in

161

with him to back his hand. With just Coulter along, he'll probably not only think twice, but three or four times."

"Yet they could try it, and I'd feel Hayfork was responsible. Grady Haskell should be warned. Would you, Sandy?"

"Of course. I'll drift back down the trail and keep an eye on things. And don't you worry, Katie. I say again, we're better off without Vince Tendler and Stack Coulter."

It was past dark when Sandy Lee got back to the ranch. Katherine was quickly to the door to answer the old rider's knock.

"No need to worry," was the succinct report. "Tendler and Coulter didn't even go to town. They took the old military trail around the head of the canyon."

This, Katherine considered soberly. "Where would they be going, I wonder?"

Sandy shrugged. "I don't know where they were going, but I know where that trail leads. Straight into the Beaverhead country—Rutt Dubison's country."

Katherine caught her breath. "Could that mean they were going over—over to—?"

"To Dubison?" supplied Sandy. "Wouldn't put it past them. Remember, Katie, what I told you about Tendler, how he wanted this ranch? Well, now that his first plan on how to get it has blown up in his face, he could be figuring another idea. And if he figures the move might get him what he wants—which is this ranch—then I don't believe he'd hesitate a second at going in with Dubison."

"What do you think we should do?"

"Sit tight, and keep our eyes and ears open. You'll need a new foreman. I recommend Jeff Keough. He's sound and dependable and the rest of the crew like and respect him. Jeff will do fine. And if anybody should get the idea that just because Vince Tendler ain't around the layout any more, Hayfork is about to fold up, they could be in for one hell of a surprise!"

Rutt Dubison's headquarters had once been a way station on the old military road reaching out into the Beaverhead country, built back in the days when Indian trouble could be expected anywhere through the Trinity Hills. But those days were long since past and the Utes and the troops that had rounded them up and subdued them, long since gone, leaving the way station deserted. This had Rutt Dubison moved in on and claimed as his own.

For his purpose it was ideal. This was wild country, hide-out country, the kind of country sought by the kind of men he wanted for his crew. They came from all four points of the compass, men wolfish like himself, gaunt from far, fast riding away from a variety of misdeeds ranging from petty thievery to brutal murder. Violent men, these, with the stain of a couched wickedness in their eyes, and ready guns at their belts.

Of such, Rutt Dubison asked but a single question. Would they ride with him and do his bidding? Beyond that, their business and their past was their own. And there were some who stayed with him and there were others who rode on, always fleeing from something they could never completely elude.

Central building of the layout was the old way station itself, which Dubison took over for his own use. Scattered round about in the timber, cabins which had once housed United States troopers were shelter for the rest of the outfit. Some of these cabins were shared by two men, others held but one, these solitary ones being men who, aside from times of action and carousing, preferred their own company to that of others.

Such a one had been Rudy Shedd. But the cabin he had held was now empty, and the man who had occupied it filled a lonely grave in the timber.

A certain deputy sheriff named Haskell had seen to this violent end of a violent man. For he had blasted the life from Rudy Shedd with a sawed-off shotgun, and afterwards this same Grady Haskell had smashed the butt of the shotgun into Rutt Dubison's face, dropping him in an unconscious heap.

These were the thoughts burning through Rutt Dubison's mind as he now slouched his lank length far down in a chair in the musty gloom of the old way station, nursing a glass of whiskey as he had nursed many others since the happenings that left him with these scorching memories.

Late afternoon held the high hill country, afternoon now moving swiftly into early evening, and in the timber the shadows were long and blue and velvety with a mellow, shifting beauty.

A man showed at the way station doorway, bringing laconic report.

"Two ridin' in."

Dubison grunted. "Who?"

"Gentile says two of the Hayfork crowd. Tendler and Coulter."

Dubison straightened in his chair.

"Maybe they're not the only ones. Have somebody ride a circle, just in case."

"Gentile already did. These are alone."

"Fair enough. Bring them in."

Dubison left his chair, lifted down a belt and holstered gun from a wall peg and buckled these about his lank middle. After which he prowled to the door and stared along the road to the east where came the new arrivals.

Here at the door, where better light could reach it,

164

Dubison's face showed strong evidence of the blow that had laid him out in Reservation's Canyon House saloon. The upper half of his features were still one great dark bruise, from which his eyes peered between swollen, heavy lids.

The two coming in were Tendler and Coulter, sure enough. When within a hundred yards of the station, armed men appeared on either side of the road, halting them. There was a short argument, after which Tendler and Coulter unbuckled their gun belts and hung them on their saddle horns. Whereupon they were allowed to advance.

Dubison went back to his chair. He heard the two ride up in front, heard their spurs jangle as they dismounted. Then they stepped in, and he had an advantage on them, for his eyes were adjusted to this deeper gloom, while theirs were not.

"Well, well," he greeted. "This surprises me. Hardly expected to ever see you two coming riding in so free and easy. You must have a reason. What is it?"

"A deal," said Tendler, his voice thick, almost guttural.

"A deal, eh? To tell the truth I'm a little suspicious of deals. Most that have been offered me left me holding the short end of things. And I don't like that."

"How'd you like to split Hayfork with me?" asked Vince Tendler bluntly, plainly driven by the impatience of anger.

Rutt Dubison did not answer right away, instead taking the time to build a cigarette as he considered. Slowly he spoke.

"I don't get it, Tendler. You and me split up Hayfork. Does that mean you're ready to sell your own outfit down the river?"

"I'm not with Hayfork any more. I quit today."

"Why?"

Tendler made an irritated gesture. "Does it matter?"

"It might. Naturally I'd wonder. This deal—what is it? I mean—just how do you figure to go about it?"

"Stack here, and me, we tie in with you," Tendler explained. "We can put our finger on every head of stock wearing the Hayfork iron. With you and your crowd working with us we can clean that outfit right down to the bone. After which we'll take over the range."

"Sounds reasonable—and attractive," Dubison admitted carefully. "And how would we split the take?"

"Twenty-five, seventy-five. Twenty-five should make it well worth your while."

"Now there it is," said Dubison. "Just what I meant about these damn deals. Always the short end for me. Well, all I can say, Tendler, there's nothing wrong with your gall. Me and my boys supply the bone and muscle while you walk off with the gravy. That don't listen a bit good to me."

"But I'm bringing you the information that will make things easy for us," Tendler argued. "You've been trying to work on Hayfork for a long time, but without any great success. I can make it easy for both of us."

"Maybe," evaded Dubison warily. "Maybe not. How do I know this ain't some kind of a trick to lead me and my boys into a trap of some sort? How do I know you're telling the truth about being through at Hayfork?"

"Ask Stack here. He'll tell you."

"Hell!" Dubison scoffed. "He can be just as big a liar as you."

Tendler turned toward the door. "Come on, Stack," he said thickly. "Let's get out of here."

"Hold it!" Dubison put solid impact behind the

166

words. "Now that you're here, you stay until I say different. Easy! I got a gun on you. If I decide you're telling the truth, then we'll make a deal, but not on any damn fool twenty-five to me and seventy-five to you."

Outside, the afternoon had run through its last swift moments and dusk was taking over. Dubison lifted a call.

"Hey, Stinger—come in here and light the lamp!"

The one who had announced the approach of Tendler and Coulter entered wordlessly, climbed on a chair and lighted a hanging lamp, then left as quickly as he had entered.

As the lamp flame took hold and grew to full size, a spreading cone of yellow light thrust downward, bringing all three of these men into its disclosing substance. Rutt Dubison's glance settled on Vince Tendler.

"Oh—oh!" he exclaimed quickly, "I begin to understand a little. Who on Hayfork gave you a whipping?"

"Nobody!" snapped Tendler.

"Well, somebody did. You look like you'd been chopping wood with your face. Who cut you down to size?"

Badgered to recklessness, Tendler blurted, "If you must know, the same one who knocked your face out of line."

In this man, Rutt Dubison, despite the rancor and hatred and avid thirst for vengeance he felt toward Grady Haskell, there lay a certain strain of sardonic humor. So now he threw back his head and gave vent to a gust of that strange, ghostly, silent laughter of his.

Vince Tendler, knowing no humor, stared. "What the hell's so funny?"

"Both of us," said Dubison. "Here we are making

167

talk about taking Hayfork apart, when neither of us could handle a single man—not at first try, anyhow. Maybe we better look at some facts, Tendler. That fellow Haskell represents law—tough law—as tough as any I ever met up with. He don't bluff, he don't scare, and he's hell wicked in a fight. So, before we make any talk about taking Hayfork apart, let's figure out a way to take care of Haskell."

Dubison took a last drag on his cigarette, tossed the butt aside.

"Yeah, Haskell's tough, like I say—but he's mortal. And until he's dead, I'm not interested in anything else. My boys feel the same way about it. He killed Rudy Shedd. He clubbed me down like I was a steer for slaughter. He took our guns and run us out of town like we were a bunch of puling bums. And neither me or my boys do anything else until we even up with that fellow."

"You got any plan figured?" Tendler asked.

Dubison nodded. "A ruckus in town at night to pull him out into the street. Boys of mine hid around here and there in good shooting range when he does show. As I say, he's mortal. One bullet in the right place is all it will take."

"When do you expect to make the try?"

"We still got some guns, but not enough. I got some more coming in. When they get here, then we hit. If you want to ride with us and see it through, then we'll talk a deal on Hayfork, on a straight fifty-fifty split. How about it?"

This was, Vince Tendler knew, the way it would have to be, whether he liked it or not. And it wasn't too bad, offering as it did a chance to get even with Haskell. And, if it should happen in the ruckus that both Haskell and Rutt Dubison ended up dead, then he, Vince Tendler, would have a proposition to offer the rest of the Beaverhead crowd. No, this idea of Dubison's wasn't at all bad.

He nodded. "I'll go with you."

13

THE NIGHT WAS a deep mystery all about and the sound of the river a steady voice through the dark. At the edge of the pool behind Joe Peele's cabin, Grady Haskell stripped and slid a lean, wiry body into the depths. First grip of the water was icy, making him reach deep for breath. Afterwards it was wild vigor and he raced up and down with slashing, driving strokes.

Panting and blowing he rolled over and with his face to the vast sweep of glittering stars let the current carry him where it would. Then he swam again and at the head of the pool climbed out and with a rough towel had his rubdown.

Squatted on his heels on the bank, Joe Peele spat a dead cigarette butt from his lips and made lugubrious observation.

"Must be mighty fine to do that and enjoy it. Was I to try, my bones would shake plumb apart."

Haskell laughed softly, vigorous with his towel.

"Not bad after the first plunge, Joe. And I needed it, else tomorrow morning I'd be so sore and stiff I'd have a time of it getting out of bed."

"You sure are a hard one to figger," grumbled Joe. "A few hours ago you stage one awful tough ruckus with Vince Tendler, yet here you are bouncing around full of hell and vinegar like some gol blamed kid. Where d'you get all that damned energy?"

Haskell grinned, climbing into his clothes.

"Must be the peaceful life I lead."

Joe snorted. "Peaceful? Now if that ain't tall siwash!" He straightened up. "Well, I got to get along and check on this and that. There's a little sorrel filly at the stable what's a cussed nuisance. Always pawing at something. Gets a leg over the halter rope, seems like, not matter how short I tie her. Keeps a man afraid she'll throw herself or get rope-burned. You put her in a box stall and she keeps pawing and banging at things until you feel like taking a pick handle to her. Was it up to me I'd put her in a corral of nights. But she's sort of a pet with Jim Kineen and he wants her kept inside."

Joe tramped away and Haskell, finished dressing, spread his towel where tomorrow's sun would dry it, lit up a cigar, then sauntered back to town.

Turning from the alley into the street he saw a match flare on the porch of Milo Jellick's store and maintain a small, short glow against the front of the place. Earlier, he had taken down the Jack Breedon notice, now that it had served its purpose, so only the Frank Gentile dodger remained. Now, by the frugal light of a match, someone was reading it.

The match flickered out and with a scuff of spur chains and clatter of boot heels a rider came swiftly off the porch and along to the Canyon House hitch rail where a solitary saddle pony stood, and left town at a storming run.

Haskell smiled sardonically. Given twenty-four hours and the word of that dodger would spread the length and breadth of the Trinity Hills country. After which, anything could happen. So much, he mused, for honor among thieves!

In the store he found Jim Kineen and Milo Jellick together. They were old cronies and in a way represented the true voice and spirit of this little hill town of Reservation. Towns such as this, reflected Haskell, had their beginnings, grew to a certain limit, then continued to exist because they always held two or three such sound, stubborn men as these. The pair of them observed him with interest.

"By rights," Jim Kineen said, "you should be in bed nursing your aches and pains."

"Maybe," agreed Haskell. "But instead I decided to get rid of them by taking a swim."

"Swim! Just now? In the river?"

"Where else?"

"Great thunder, man—you lost your mind?"

Haskell grinned. "I hope not."

"But that water's like ice."

"Not quite. Call it brisk."

"Brisk?" Kineen gave a vicarious shiver. "Now I know why you were able to handle Tendler. You're not ordinary flesh—you're rawhide, plumb! Can you imagine such a thing, Milo—a man jumping into that river water of his own free will, at night, and just for the hell of it? Br-r-r!"

"I must admit my imagination doesn't reach quite that far," Jellick admitted dryly. He put a keen glance on Haskell. "Something I can imagine, though, and when I consider it I turn uneasy. For you, Friend Haskell, are not one I'd care to see dead."

Startled, Haskell said, "That has a damned funny sound. I wasn't figuring on dying just yet."

"No man does until the bullet hits him. And if ever anyone invited such, you're the man. Between Rutt Dubison and now Vince Tendler, I don't like the odds on your future."

Haskell's eyes narrowed slightly and he drew deeply on his cigar.

"There's the possibility, of course, and I'd be a

jackfool not to recognize it. Yet, somehow I don't quite see it in Vince Tendler. With Dubison, likely enough, for from what I saw of him he shapes up as all two-legged wolf. On the other hand, while Tendler is arrogant and overbearing and with a strong strain of the brute in him, I don't see him as a cold blooded killer."

"If he isn't," declared Jellick flatly, "then I never saw one who was. How about that, Jim?"

Kineen nodded sagely, fixing Haskell with a shrewd, puckered survey and speaking with deep seriousness.

"My friend, I've high regard for your fighting abilit, but little enough for your judgment if you mean what you say about Tendler. You were not close around when he got his senses back, so you did not see the look of him or the way he acted when he pulled out of town. Milo and I did. And never was there a man more crazy, killing mad. You say he was arrogant, which is true enough, and when you shame an arrogant one as you shamed Vince Tendler then you have made a mortal, hating, unforgiving enemy."

"And I," put in Milo Jellick, "seem to recall him grabbing for his gun when you began getting him on the hip. If his holster hadn't been empty at the moment, there's no telling how that ruckus would have ended."

Musing through another quiet moment, Haskell shrugged.

"What must be, will be. I hope the two of you realize now how much trouble could have been avoided if you'd been willing to talk earlier, instead of dodging all around the blueberry patch?"

Kineen nodded. "We realize it. We have from the first. But it was not our proper place to talk. It was best that you learn the truth from Katie Levening. Which you now have."

"It seems," probed Haskell, "there was a fight, a shootout between Miss Levening's father and Deputy Jack Breedon. I'll have to know all about that. What can you tell me?"

"Only that Breedon was killed and Levening near so. One man can give you the whole picture. Sandy Lee. He was there."

"So Miss Levening told me. Well, I'll be riding out to Hayfork in the morning, and I'll listen to Sandy Lee then. You're sure there's nothing you want to add?"

"There's this," Milo Jellick supplied, with some emphasis. "Jim Levening is as fine a man as ever lived. While that fellow Breedon, like it or not, was a damned scoundrel, a disgrace to the star he'd once worn."

"Once worn?"

"That's right—once worn. For he took it off and threw it away after he started running hog wild with Frank Gentile and the rest of Rutt Dubison's outfit."

A cold gleam tightened Haskell's eyes. "You're making a large sized statement, Jellick. You got proof to back it up, proof that Jack Breedon turned renegade?"

"Only the word of men whose word is good. Jim Kineen's, Amos Potter's, Sandy Lee's—my own. If you can believe us, then you have your proof."

Haskell's cigar had gone out. With slow care he got it alight and drawing well again, all the while considering the flat statement Milo Jellick had made. It was a two edged thing. Though it cast a shadow across the integrity of the law as entrusted to one man, it also opened wide the door of conjecture, disclosing possibilities which could explain many things.

He moved to the door and looked out into the night. Star shine on the dust of the street struck up a reflected silver glow and in the throat of the canyon the river beat out its sonorous rumble. A little wind, whipping in through the dark, brought with it the clean wildness of the high peaks.

Haskell spoke across his shoulder.

"Gentlemen, you have given me something to think about. Obliged, and—goodnight!"

He was up and tramping along to Jim Kineen's feed stable the following morning before the rest of the town was astir. Mrs. Wall had fixed him early breakfast in the hotel kitchen and the lingering goodness of it was a flavor on his tongue along with that of the day's first cigarette.

At the stable the blaze-faced dun whickered eager greeting, which earned it a quick brushing down before being saddled. Vinegary from inactivity, the horse fretted at the bit, and as soon as he was clear of town, Haskell let it run. Half a mile of this against the quickening lift of the hill road took the edge off, and the dun settled into an easy trail gait of half jog, half fast walk. Thereafter, Haskell put all thought and attention on what this day might hold.

On turning in the night before he had lain awake some little time, assaying all the factors of the past eventful hours. He had carefully considered the advice and warnings of Jim Kineen and Milo Jellick, and knew that it was good. So now his eyes and ears were working all the time, and when he topped out into the country where the high meadows ran, he took to the timber, paralleling the road. And presently, in the same meadow where he had met with Katherine Levening the first time he rode this way, it was Sandy Lee who sat a patient saddle, shoulders hunched against the chill, pipe smoke curling about his grizzled head.

When Haskell left the timber and came across the meadow to him, Sandy nodded approvingly.

"Wise," he said briefly. "Way things are stacking up in these hills, a man can't be too careful. Katie said you'd be coming along and sent me to meet you."

"You know why I'm here, of course," Haskell said.

"I know. You want a look at Jim Levening. And I reckon also you'd like to see where that Breedon feller is buried?"

"That's right."

"Then," Sandy said, "we might as well ride out there, first. Jim Levening ain't going to get away from you. You heard the shape he's in?"

"Yes. I understand you saw the shootout between him and Breedon?"

"I saw it. When we get where it happened, I'll give it to you exactly the way it was."

They left the meadow and presently Sandy swung into a dim trace running west across the hills.

"Old military road," he explained. "Heads out past the canyon into the Beaverhead country. And it was along this that Breedon and a Beaverhead rider named Gentile were making off with near twenty head of Hayfork beef when Jim Levening and me caught up with them."

"You mean," demanded Haskell, "that they were rustling Hayfork cattle?"

"I sure don't mean nothing else," Sandy declared vehemently. "And not the first time, either. Rutt Dubison and the Beaverhead crowd been working on our stuff every chance they get, which is why there's no love lost between them and us. Facts are, things have been building toward a showdown for a long time,

177

and it could come any day, now that Vince Tendler has pulled out."

"What's that! Tendler—he's left Hayfork?"

"Him and Coulter. Yesterday afternoon he was trying to get the crew to ride back to town with him and get you—get you once and for all—was the way he put it. Katie, she lit into him good, told him she'd not stand for anything of the sort, and that any Hayfork hand who moved against you now, was through, fired. Tendler, he said all right then, he was through, and him and Coulter rode out.

"Well, I kept an eye on them and they didn't head for town after all. Instead they turned off along this way we're on now. Tendler had made talk that if he was through, then Hayfork was going to be through, too. Which, with him heading for Beaverhead country, kind of suggests maybe he's out to move in with Rutt Dubison."

"I can understand him wanting to hang my hide up to dry," Haskell observed. "The rest I don't get."

Sandy shrugged. "It's always been Tendler's ambition to some day own Hayfork. I got it figgered that he believed Katie Levening would some day marry him, which would give him the ranch. Knowing now that would never happen, he's out to go after Hayfork any way he can, rustle us blind, bust up our crew, run us out of the hills complete. Alone, or just with Coulter, he wouldn't have a chance. But with Dubison working with him, maybe. Sure I'm guessing, but it could be something like that."

"Yes, it could," Haskell agreed. "How many head of cattle does Hayfork run?"

Sandy considered, frowning.

"There ain't been a range count lately, what with things being upset the way they are. But off-hand, I'd say between thirty-five hundred and four thousand head."

"Which," said Haskell, definitely startled, "makes Hayfork a pretty sizable outfit."

"Sure it is. It's no two-bit spread, not by a jugful. It's plenty fat to make any damn cow rustler's mouth water. You yourself saw Hayfork cattle over on Rancheria Creek. Well, we got 'em running further east than that."

They had been keeping to a steady pace along this old military road, now badly grown over, as it skirted slopes and crossed ridge points and dipped through thickly timbered hollows. Abruptly it broke into a small, open basin some three hundred yards across. Sandy reined up.

"Here's the place," he said quietly. "Here's where it all happened, right here in this little basin."

Twisting up a cigarette, Haskell looked the place over. This was a lonely, isolated spot where tragedy had struck; where one man had found death and another nearly so.

"All right," he said presently. "Let's have the story."

"Like I said, Jim Levening and me, we were trailing this little bunch of cattle," Sandy explained. "We'd picked up the first sign back where the cattle had been bunched. We knew it was a rustling deal, with Hayfork cattle being driven out this direction, and we could see that two riders were pulling the steal. We caught up with 'em there."

Sandy paused and pointed.

"The cattle were yonder, moving along pretty well. This feller Breedon, and the other one, Gentile, were both riding drag, but spread out so they could cut quick up the flanks, should a critter make a try to break out that way. Jim and me, we come into the

179

open right where you and me are now. Breedon, he turned to holler something to Gentile just as Jim and me showed, and he saw us. He yanked a rifle out of a scabbard, quick as a wink and started to cut down on us."

Sandy drew a deep breath, as though in the telling he was again living through a deadly episode.

"Yeah," he repeated, "this Breedon, he started throwing lead our way as fast as he could swing the lever of his rifle. Jim Levening, thinking way out ahead of me, began shooting back. Gentile, he didn't even try and fight; he just busted and run for it, riding low and hard. Time I got into action he was already ducking into the timber. I chucked a couple of shots in his direction just for luck, but didn't do no good.

"Well, sir—right about then it's Jim Levening's horse that comes spookin' by me, under an empty saddle. I turn and look for Jim and there he is, spread out on the ground. And yonder, where the cattle were beginning to scatter, there's another horse without a rider, and this feller Breedon, he's down on the ground, too."

"You hadn't shot at Breedon at all?" Haskell asked.

Sandy shook his head. "Not none, I was trying for Gentile."

"And Gentile did no shooting or tried to fight back in any way?"

"Not any. He just rode for it and kept on riding. He must have figgered there was more than just me and Jim Levening on the trail, and he didn't want no part of an argument with them kind of odds."

"What did you do next?"

"Why, I shucked out of my saddle and run over to Jim Levening. His eyes were wide open and he could look at me, but he couldn't seem to speak or move. He was shot through the body, low down. He was alive, but I couldn't see him with a ghost of a chance, hit the way he was.

"Well, there's a spring yonder in the timber and I went over there for a hatful of water. On the way I had to pass close to Breedon. One look was enough to tell he was as dead as he'd ever be. So I brought water to Jim Levening, tied him up as best I could, got him across his saddle and took him home. I was sure he'd be dead, time I got there. But he wasn't. And somehow, by the grace of God and the help of Doc Venable, it looks now that he'll make the grade all the way back."

"What about Breedon?"

Sandy shrugged. "Me and some of the boys, we came back after the cattle. We brought along some tools and buried Breedon yonder at the edge of the timber."

They rode over to the spot. Grady Haskell looked down at a long, narrow rectangle of slightly mounded earth, already beginning to sod over with new grass. There was no marker of any sort and, given another season or two, no trace of the grave would remain. Guessing at Haskell's thoughts, Sandy said:

"Mebbe we weren't too Christian about the way we dug the hole and put him in it, but right about then the only man we had on our minds was Jim Levening."

Throughout it all, Grady Haskell knew he'd been listening to a recital of stark truth. For there had been a simplicity and guilelessness in Sandy's every word which could not have been dreamed up or fabricated in any way.

Beyond doubt, under this rectangle of disturbed earth, lay a man who had gone bad, who had turned renegade, dishonoring his star and the oath that had permitted him to wear it. For a reason, perhaps, no one would ever know.

Haskell reined the dun around.

"We'll get along to Hayfork headquarters, now."

They made the ride without incident and for the most part in silence. As they came up the long meadow, Haskell nodded an indicating head.

"As pretty a setting for a ranch headquarters as I ever saw. I can understand Tendler's wishes to own it."

"Me, too," admitted Sandy. "But I don't like his ideas on how to get hold of it. Not worth a damn, I don't!"

They topped the slope and moved in on the buildings. Katherine Levening, crisp and pretty in a simple gingham house dress, stepped from the ranchhouse door. Her greeting was grave and direct.

"I've been waiting for you," she told Haskell. "Come in, please."

Leading his horse, Sandy Lee cut away toward the corrals. Grady Haskell followed this slim, raven-haired girl into the house, deciding that she had never looked better than at this moment. Always before there had been the shadow of strain in the depths of her eyes, as if she were a hunted being, fearful and desperate. Now her eyes were clear and quiet and she seemed at ease.

She led the way across a large, restful living room, along a short hall, then paused at a door opening off this.

"In here," she said softly. "He is sleeping, which Doctor Venable says is the one best medicine for him. You will think him a mere shadow of a man, but he is much better than he was. I have seen the gain, day by day, and last night he whispered my name. My father, Mr. Haskell, is going to be a well man again. I hope the law will wait until that time before taking him into custody. Come!"

The sick room was shadowed and Haskell had to stand close to the bedside to get clear view of the face of the man lying there. It was a gaunt face, all bony angles and deep hollows, the face of one who had gone far down into the depths before beginning the desperate climb back.

"Sandy shaved him last night," the daughter murmured. "When it was done, he smiled. You—you've no idea what it meant to me to see that smile."

Again Haskell studied the face on the pillow. Despite its present gaunt fragility it contained a strong certainty of character and worth. As if confirming a conclusion previously arrived at, Haskell nodded as he turned away.

"Thank you," he said, "for letting me see him."

Back in the living room Katherine Levening confronted Grady Haskell with just a trace of her old anxiety.

"Well?"

"I'm wondering," he said soberly, "why you feared the law so much?"

"I—we—how do you mean?"

He shrugged.

"First it was you, searching my gear for evidence of my real identity. Then it was Tendler and others giving me a gang beating on the mistaken theory that such would run me out of the hills. The first time I rode up this way, you met me first, worried and fearful and afterwards Sandy Lee dusted up the road with rifle lead to convince me I'd best turn back to town. Finally, no matter who I asked, I could get no straight answers on Jack Breedon. And none of that mumbo-jumbo was necessary."

She was watching him with a still intentness. "I yet don't understand."

"Why," explained Haskell, "it's like this. Knowing what I do now, I doubt the law will hold your father to any account other than a factual report of the matter to go down in the records as reason for and certainty of, Breedon's death. For, regardless of what Jack Breedon might have been at one time, the day he was killed he was a cattle rustler, consorting on friendly terms with the very man he'd come into the hills after—Frank Gentile. Not only that, but when caught in the act, he began the shooting. And of course your father had every right to shoot back."

"What proof have you that all this was so?"

"Sandy Lee's word—the word of an eye-witness."

"And you're accepting it?"

"Certainly: Sandy Lee is the sort who couldn't lie convincingly if his life depended on it."

The swift brightness of tears touched her eyes and she turned her back on Haskell for a moment, busy with a wisp of handkerchief. When again she faced him her smile was tremulous, her voice a trifle uncertain.

"I—I'm sorry. Don't mind me. But after all the fear and worry, the relief is so great—!" She used the handkerchief again, then went on more steadily. "You see, though we knew the truth all along, it seemed to us to be much too pat and glib for the law ever to believe it. All we could see was the fact that my father had killed a man who had come into these hills a deputy sheriff, and we were certain the sheriff's office at Ordeville would investigate and hold us to grim account for it. You—you really believe the law will be—lenient?"

"Sure of it. No cow country jury would ever hold your father for the killing of a cattle rustler, nor would any sheriff as shrewd and sensible as Bill Hoe arrest him for it. I would say your only real concern now should be for your father's full recovery and for any possible trouble Vince Tendler might be stirring up for Hayfork."

She exclaimed softly. "You knew Vince was no longer riding for us?"

"He and Coulter," Haskell nodded. "Sandy told me about it. Also the exact reason why Tendler was fired."

She flushed. "It was something bound to come. Matters had been building toward it for a long time. It's a relief to have it settled."

"Sandy," went on Haskell, "also told me Tendler made some threats about hitting back at Hayfork. And that after leaving, he and Coulter headed for the Beaverhead country. Maybe that means mischief."

"It does if he makes a deal with Rutt Dubison. Anything could happen, then."

"It would seem those fellows could all stand a little more convincing," Haskell observed. "Made to realize cattle rustling and sundry other odds and ends of devilment are frowned on by responsible channels of authority. I may be riding out that way in a few days. If so, I'll have a little talk with them on the matter."

"No!" She said it quickly, Katherine Levening did. "No. That wouldn't be at all wise, you riding into that country alone. Not after all that has happened. Rutt Dubison has some very vicious men riding with him."

"How about Tendler. Do you figure him the same, now?"

She nodded soberly. "Very much so. I—I thought I knew him fairly well. I know now that I've never known the real Vince Tendler at all."

"You say there are vicious ones with Dubison. We agree on that," Haskell said. "And I'm after one of

185

them. Mister Frank Gentile. He is another reason why I'm in these hills. He's wanted for all the reasons stated in the dodger on Jellick's store, and if the truth were known, probably for a lot more. A thoroughly undesirable citizen, Mister Gentile. I'm waiting a time to see if the bait offered by the dodger gets any results. If not, then I go after him."

She eyed him gravely. "Nothing frightens you, does it?"

"Nothing frightens me!" His grin was quick, setting up a nest of wrinkles at his eye corners. "Girl, you just don't know. You couldn't be more wrong. Plenty of things scare me to death. But," he added, the grin fading to a sober musing, "I guess the greatest fear of all for a man in my job, is the fear of being afraid. So, we bow our necks and go ahead."

He began moving toward the door and she spoke swiftly.

"Even if you had breakfast before you left town, it had to be an early one. Perhaps another cup of coffee about now—?"

"You save my life!" he agreed with alacrity.

She led the way into the kitchen where, as with the rest of the house, the mark of a deft feminine touch and an instinct for orderliness and comfort was apparent. Haskell took a chair at the oil cloth covered table and watched her, quiet with his thoughts.

She poured the coffee and sat across from him.

"They must be interesting to take you so far away," she observed. "Your thoughts, I mean."

"Not as far as you think," he said. "If you're interested, I'll share them."

"Please!"

"Very well. I was thinking how truly pleasant it was to be in this kitchen, drinking coffee with you."

She laughed softly, coloring. "At least that was the polite thing to say."

"And gospel," he affirmed. "Just as was something else I once told you. How, for me at least, one moment during our first meeting in my room, was a very pleasant one."

She colored again, more deeply. "You won't let me forget that, will you?"

"Why should I, when I can't forget it myself."

He drained his cup, stood up, reaching for his smoking.

"I think, Katie Levening, I better get out of here, else I'll be saying more than I should. You are a dangerous person to be around. You unlock a man's tongue, make him commit himself past his own good judgment."

She did not try and hold him further, but as she stood in the open door, watching him swing into his saddle and ride away, far back in her eyes lay a shadowed smiling.

14

MID-AFTERNOON SUN burned down on the Beaverhead country. In the way station several tables of draw poker held the interest of Rutt Dubison, Vince Tendler and a number of Dubison's crew. In an outer cabin which Dubison has assigned to him and Tendler, Stack Coulter was alone, sprawled on a bunk, arms folded beneath his head, a half burned cigarette sagging at the corner of his mouth. He was staring up at the smoke darkened pole rafters and split shakes of the place, but seeing none of it. At this moment he was a vastly troubled man and growing steadily more so as his thoughts took him on and on.

Basically, despite a hard featured appearance and a bullying swagger which he affected when he felt he could get away with it, Stack Coulter was weak. He would join with others in ganging up on a lone man, if he thought there would be small cost to himself, as had been the case against Grady Haskell, and too, he would collar someone much older and physically weaker than himself, such as Joe Peele, and from the safe vantage of a saddle on a running horse, drag him in helplessness along the street of Reservation.

Also was he the sort to make offensive advances to a girl like Ruby Peele, feeling that because she was a chore girl about the hotel, and daughter of a man classed as the town drunk, there was little danger of her having an able defender to call him to account.

It was inevitable that such as he also fawn on authority. Which had been his attitude toward Vince Tendler while Tendler was ramroding Hayfork. To be in Tendler's favor meant not only easier working assignments and other such advantages, but also it represented a measure of defense. For in Coulter's eyes, Vince Tendler had been the strong man of the east end of the Trinity Hills, and to ride at his shoulder was to share in that strength.

Which was the way it had been not too many hours ago. Now the picture was vastly changed. No longer was Vince Tendler ramroding Hayfork with arrogant, unquestioned power, nor was he the strong man with a reputation to make others get off the trail when he came along. Grady Haskell, the deputy sheriff, had taken care of all that.

Coulter stirred restlessly under the whip of his thoughts. He threw aside his cigarette butt, got upon one elbow to roll a fresh smoke, mumbling a peevish curse as he spilled some of his tobacco.

This spot he was now in, he didn't like at all. Why, he wondered moodily, had he been fool enough to side with Tendler when Katherine Levening laid down her ultimatum? Why had he thrown away a good job to ride off with Tendler to this? Habit, maybe, having traveled so long in Tendler's shadow he hadn't thought fast enough to get out of it. And the sense of security Tendler's company had always furnished him before, was entirely gone, now.

No longer did he own a bunk in the Hayfork bunkhouse, in the good world of that ranch, where a man ate well and slept warm and knew the comfort of living among sound, dependable men. For here, in this camp of Rutt Dubison's, he was in a camp of wolves.

Every man he had so far met with here had looked him over with sullen, suspicious wariness and then left

190

him severely alone. Nor was Vince Tendler the same man he had been. Now he was rough, short of temper, and consumed with a certain malign purpose which locked him away in a savage indifference. All of which worried Stack Coulter and made him fearful.

In this kind of world he knew he would never find any ease again; too much of it was based on outlawry and destruction. As for instance the thing looming in the immediate future, the thing that might come of any given night—even this one just ahead—the raid on Reservation to get that deputy, Grady Haskell.

Rutt Dubison had made it plain that he moved in no other direction until this little item of business had been taken care of, and Vince Tendler had agreed. And Stack Coulter knew that here was something he wanted no part of, no part at all. Rutt Dubison and Vince Tendler might not care what the sure consequences of such a raid would be, Dubison and his followers being all renegade anyhow, and Tendler willing to go to any extreme to buy Dubison's support in an all-out strike against Hayfork. But he, Stack Coulter, had his own future to consider.

As yet, he had committed no actual crime that could turn the law and public conscience entirely against him. But just let him participate in an armed raid on Reservation, regardless of cause or purpose and forever more he would be one of the hunted. For every solid man in the country would be up in arms and, even if he lived through the raid, his life would be forfeit to the first man to draw a bead on him.

The pressure of such thoughts sent a slime of sweat across Coulter's brow and cheeks, and he wiped it away with a scrubbing forearm. He got off the bunk and crossed to the open door and looked out, surveying the way station and several of the other cabins scattered among the pines. Nowhere did he see any movement. Men were either playing poker in the main building, or were lounging and sleeping in their cabins through this heat of the day.

Sudden eagerness straightened Coulter's back and put a gleam in his eye. Why not? Real security was not here or never would be. Real security was back in that other world he'd been stupid enough to leave; back at Hayfork headquarters where those good men rode, and at Reservation where other good men like Jim Kineen and Amos Potter and Milo Jellick bespoke the voice of the town and where a deputy sheriff named Grady Haskell walked the street and threw a shadow far higher and wider than Vince Tendler or Rutt Dubison ever had.

How could he regain that security now so suddenly precious? How more simply, Coulter reasoned, than by carrying word of the intended raid to Grady Haskell and the citizens of town? This must surely return him to the good graces of all worthwhile people—even regain him a place on the Hayfork crew again.

What matter that on the day he had dragged Joe Peele, Grady Haskell had whipped him down into the dust of Reservation's street? Sure he had hated Haskell for that, but if siding now with what Haskell represented would win back for him the secure world he craved, then nothing else mattered.

He took another look around, a longer and more careful one. The world lay still, as before. Faintly stirring air, vanguard of the breeze that would pick up toward evening, brought with it the far off scolding of a pine squirrel and the strong, baked resin scent of the timber. These things cemented his desperate resolve.

He turned back into the cabin, buckled on his gunbelt and donned his hat. From his warbag he pocketed what odds and ends he could carry with him without arousing suspicion in case he met up with one of the

Beaverhead crowd over at the corrals. Until he was clear of and well away from this place, it was smart to make every move as casual and innocent appearing as possible.

Even so, as sauntering he circled to the corrals which stood off a little distance to the east, the sweat of tension stung his face and his head swung and his eyes darted, back and forth and round about. He reached the corrals without incident, neither meeting or seeing anyone, and he leaned against the fence for a little time while some of the tension ran out of him.

Afterwards he moved swiftly, catching and saddling. He led his horse back into the edge of the timber before mounting. He rode a fairly wide circle through the timber to strike the old military road well to the east, and once on this, with a surge of exulting relief, he spurred for the head of Reservation Canyon and the trail which cut down the west rim of it to the town far distant below.

The moment Stack Coulter disappeared in the timber, a man stepped from behind an old log feed shed, to catch and saddle even more swiftly than Coulter had done. It was one of the things which marked Frank Gentile, the cat-like ease and swiftness with which he could move. A dark, smooth-faced man of medium size, he was one whose every action and look held that feline quality. He had the wary restlessness and sleekness and the pale, blank, unrevealing eyes, always glowing far back with the flame of an instinctive, killing cruelty.

Once in the saddle, he dropped down slope from headquarters, striking a narrow east-west trail, then spurring east along it at a driving run.

By the time Stack Coulter reached the head of Reservation Canyon and started down the rim trail with no sound or sign of pursuit or alarm stirring behind him, he felt he'd won his gamble. Every step his horse took was carrying him that much closer to security, and so his confidence grew to the point where he slowed his mount to a walk while he spun up another smoke. As he completed this his horse abruptly stopped, and Coulter looked up to find another rider blocking the trail ahead, a dark, smooth-faced rider up on a horse still blowing from hard running. A man with blank, cruel, feline eyes.

Coulter named him with a dismayed ejaculation.

"Gentile!"

"Right! And wondering where you're heading, Coulter—and why?"

Moving mechanically, Stack Coulter went to put his cigarette in his mouth, but the sudden desperate tension in his fingers crumpled the cigarette into a fluff of tobacco grains and fragmented brown paper.

"Got restless—laying around." The words came jerkily, tight and strained in his throat. "Just thought I'd take a little ride."

He tried to keep both his glance and his voice steady, but succeeded in neither. And far back in Frank Gentile's eyes a feline glow became hotter and more merciless.

"Why ride this way, Coulter—and in such a rush? I had to spur like hell to head you off. Now would you be heading for town?"

"Just—just riding." It was the weakest sort of an excuse, which Stack Coulter well knew, but he could think of nothing better in the extreme of the moment. Those damn, blank cat's eyes of Gentile's—they hypnotized a man, so he couldn't think straight or talk straight, either.

"You're lying!" Gentile purred flatly. "I watched you leave headquarters. You sneaked out like a sheep-killing dog. You're up to something, Coulter. I understand there's a reward dodger up on the front of Jellick's store, offering five hundred dollars for my hide. Would that be interesting you—would you maybe be figuring on trying to sell a little information about me to that deputy, Haskell? Or would it be a warning on what Dubison is figuring for Mister Haskell?"

"I say—I'm just out for the ride," Coulter repeated dully.

Frank Gentile was all renegade, born that way, a two legged predator to whom outlawry came as natural as breathing. There was neither conscience or mercy in him, and he took a vicious pride in his ability to bring out the fear in other men. It was that way now.

"You're lying," he charged again. "And I'm taking you back to headquarters. We'll see what you have to say when Rutt Dubison starts asking you questions. He'll get the true answers if he has to cut you in half with a quirt!"

Sweat burned down Stack Coulter's face, stung his eyes. His lips were dry and he ran his tongue across them. Dismal, fatalistic foreboding came to him. There was no easy way out of this. He shivered to think what could lie for him back at Dubison's headquarters. But past Frank Gentile, a few miles on down trail, lay a beckoning security. There was but one way to reach it.

Desperate cunning come to Stack Coulter, the cunning of a self-centered man, scheming for what was literally his life.

"All right," he shrugged, leaning as if to knee his horse around. "If that's the way you want it, that's the way it will be. We'll go back and see what Dubison has to say."

With these words he went for his gun.

Stack Coulter was as good as the average at this sort of thing, good enough to feel he had at least an even chance of getting there first. It was the final mistake of his life.

Coldly alert and suspecting something of the sort, Frank Gentile's gun was out and smashing its hard report before Coulter's weapon was fully clear of the leather. Coulter's horse, having started a swing, kept on with the move, but as it completed the turn, it no longer carried a rider.

In town, Grady Haskell spent much of the afternoon in his room, frowning in concentration as he wrote out a lengthy report for Bill Hoe. So far as he could he gave full account of what had happened to Jack Breedon, and why. He did as objective a job as possible, keeping personal feeling and conjecture out of it, giving only the facts as he had found them. He offered one suggestion, however, which was that Breedon's record, before he became a deputy, be looked into.

The report done, signed and sealed in an envelope for mailing, Haskell leaned back in his chair, yawning and stretching mightily. He got to his feet, restless in the trapped heat of this upper story room. From the open window he looked down and over town. This was the season when late summer was turning to early fall, and even here, high in these lofty hills, there came days such as this one, when the sun laid a still and smothering touch across the world.

He stretched again, the hard angles of his face softening in a gentle musing. It had been a real comfort to drink coffee with Katie Levening in the cheery kitchen of the Hayfork ranchhouse. There had been an atmosphere of intimacy which made it an easy picture to remember and a satisfying one to think about.

In sudden echo came the rataplan of hoofs at the west end of the street, and then it was Sandy Lee who came speeding in. He hauled up at Jellick's store and ran inside. There was a sense of urgency here which set Haskell to wondering, so he caught up his letter and hat and hurried down. As he moved into the open of the street, Sandy showed on the store porch, spied him and came quickly to meet him.

"Looking for you," Sandy said.

"Trouble at the ranch, maybe?" Haskell asked swiftly.

"Not at the ranch, but on the west side canyon trail. A dead man there."

"Who?"

"Stack Coulter. And from what I saw it must have been Frank Gentile who killed him."

Haskell considered this word for a somber moment, then tipped his head. "Let's get in out of this sun while you tell me about it."

They moved into the warm shade of the store's overhang.

"It's like this," Sandy explained. "Katie Levening, she's made Jeff Keough foreman, and Jeff and me, we figgered it wouldn't hurt none to keep check on things, just in case Tendler meant all those threats he made. So I'm out scouting the old military road around the head of the canyon. I spot this rider coming in from the direction of Beaverhead. He's moving right along and watching some over his shoulder like he was mebbe afraid of being followed. When he gets closer I see it's Stack Coulter.

"Well, he turns into the west rim trail which leads down here to town. He ain't out of sight more'n a couple of minutes, seems to me, when I hear a single shot down there. I'm trying to figure what that could have meant when here comes Frank Gentile up the trail and lining out for Beaverhead.

"I let him get well out of sight then I ride down to take a look. I don't go over a couple of hundred yards when I meet up with Coulter's horse. A little past that, there's Stack himself, piled up by the trail."

"And dead?"

"Plenty!" Sandy said emphatically. "He's too big and heavy for me to handle by myself, so I tie his bronc close by and head for town to find you."

Haskell nodded grimly. "We must go after him, of course."

"I figured you'd feel that way," Sandy said.

"As soon as I mail this letter," Haskell said.

It was well after dark by the time they got back to town and turned the body of Stack Coulter over to Doc Venable at his office down street west of the hotel. It had been a grisly chore, one which left Grady Haskell depressed both mentally and physically. He craved hot coffee or a good jolt of whiskey or some such to lift him out of his bleakness of spirit. He would never, he decided, become calloused toward violent death, when dealt either by himself or by another.

At the hotel, supper was a full hour past, a fact which Joe Peele noted when Haskell and Sandy Lee brought Haskell's dun and the stocky bay Coulter had ridden, to the stable for the night.

"You fellers got to eat," Joe declared. "Come on along to my cabin. I ain't had evening grub yet, myself, and there's a pot of mulligan on the back of the stove that my girl Ruby fixed."

So presently they were in Joe's humble dwelling, eating a late and welcome supper. They discussed the killing frugally, hazarding various guesses as to the reason for it.

"Only one thing I know for sure," declared Joe Peele finally. "There ain't ever going to be any real quiet in these hills until that Beaverhead outfit is busted up and scattered. Ain't a single one of them worth hell room, and that goes for anybody who joins in with them. Mebbe I should feel sorry for Stack Coulter, but remembering that day he set out to drag me along the street, I just don't."

Done with the meal, Haskell rolled a smoke, and, after thanking Joe, he and Sandy Lee cut back to the street.

"I might as well put for home," Sandy said.

"And keep on watching the trails," Haskell suggested. "If you come up with anything worthwhile, let me know."

Sandy headed off down street to where he had left his horse in front of Doc Venable's office. Haskell turned into the store where, with no surprise, he found Milo Jellick and Jim Kineen hob-nobbing as usual. They asked immediately for all the word on Coulter's killing, and Haskell gave it to them briefly.

"It's the start," Jellick said.

Haskell looked at him narrowly. "Start of what?"

"That which has long been shaping up in these hills—a showdown between the right kind of people and the wrong kind. It's a thing I've had a feeling about. That on a certain day, some sign, such as a dead man in the trail, could mean the start. Like the first wild gust of an approaching storm."

"Maybe," said Haskell skeptically. "But it's simpler to figure it just one renegade gunning down another. For some personal reason, probably a damn small one. For it doesn't take much to set off a killer of Gentile's stripe."

"Simpler," put in Jim Kineen, his eyes puckered and shrewdly considering. "And it could be just that. Yet there are other angles that grow steadily wider as you look at them. This fellow Coulter is plainly heading for town, as the west rim trail leads no place else. He's in a hurry and concerned with his back trail. From the sign as you and Sandy Lee read it when you went out for the body, Gentile had come in across the flank of the hills to head Coulter off. These, my friend, are the facts?"

"The facts," Haskell admitted. "Stay with them."

"Very well," went on Kineen. "Each by itself could mean little. Put them together—the why of them, I mean—and you could come up with something plenty big. Such as maybe Coulter was bringing some kind of word to town which Gentile didn't want known— maybe a warning of some kind."

Haskell gave a short laugh. "You should put a halter on that imagination, Jim. Else you'll be trying to fly without wings. Answer me this question. Who would Coulter have wanted to warn—and what of?"

"You, perhaps," shot back Kineen quickly. "Coulter had been at Beaverhead, and plainly enough was sneaking away from there. Would you be forgetting who is at Beaverhead? Rutt Dubison and his crowd. And now Vince Tendler, so I understand. Do you think any of them would ever forget what you did to them, how you handled them and shamed their perverted pride? If so, you should think again."

"But why would Coulter bring me a warning?" Haskell argued. "He's reason to hate me as much as any. Besides, there's long been a feud between Hayfork and the Beaverhead crowd. Gentile is Beaverhead, Coulter was Hayfork. That could be the answer to the shootout."

"True," agreed Kineen. "Yet he was ever a sly one, was Stack Coulter, where his own hide was concerned. They tell me he went over to Beaverhead with Tendler. Maybe he didn't like what he found there. Maybe he decided there was little future for Stack Coulter with that crowd, and was figuring on a deal that would get him back in the good graces of worth while folk. I tell you, the man was a schemer."

"All of that," nodded Milo Jellick. "But regardless of the why of it, the cold fact is that Frank Gentile shot Stack Coulter to death and left him where he fell. It is the demonstration of willingness to kill that is the sign, that tells the mood. It is an uneasy world, I say."

While Haskell pondered these thoughts, spurs rattled across the warped porch planks and then it was Sandy Lee again, slipping in at the door. He was grave and taut as he put his glance and words straight to Haskell.

"Queer goings on outside. When you and me come in from Joe Peele's a little bit ago, the street seemed plumb empty, with my bronc the only one at a hitch rail. It still is the only horse on the street, and between it and us four here, there's at least half a dozen men. I didn't get a close look at any of them, for they're skulking close in the shadows. I don't know what they're up to, but I got a funny feelin' along my spine. I wish I had the rifle that's slung in my saddle boot!"

"You see," said Milo Jellick quickly, turning to Haskell.

"No," retorted Haskell, "I don't, just yet. But I will."

He moved for the door. Jim Kineen, earnest and worried, stepped quickly to stop him.

"Not too fast, boy—not too fast! They could be laying for you!"

Haskell pushed by.

"If anybody is looking for me, I'll oblige them. I said it before, I say it again. The time comes when I'm afraid to carry a star along any street, in daylight or dark, that minute the star comes off—for good. For the present I'm still wearing it!"

He stood in the doorway, testing the night. Baking out of walls and roofs and the dust of the street, some of day's past warmth still clung, though a coolness had begun to steal up from the river. Stars glittered vastly, their light striking strong contrast between deep shadow at building corners, and streaks of silver glow in the open areas.

So far as Haskell could see, no one was abroad along the street, no movement anywhere, and he wondered at the word Sandy Lee had brought. One thing was certain; Sandy Lee was too old a hand to conjure substance out of nothing and be spooked by it. Sandy had seen something which called for investigation.

With the thought he wheeled sharply from the doorway into the dark beyond, and only this abrupt turn from light to dark, saved him from being dropped in his tracks.

For down street, across from the hotel, a pencil of gun flame stabbed the night. Hard, coughing report pounded out, and the bullet which would have caught him belt high and squarely, instead smashed into the door post.

He went the length of the porch and off the end of it at a crouching rush, swinging into the shelter of the alley beyond.

Behind him sounded Jim Kineen's long howl of Irish anger and then the store light went out. Came too, now, Sandy Lee's anxious call.

"Haskell—Grady—you all right?"

Sandy got his answer, but not from Haskell. Instead it echoed along the street in a man's savage shout.

"Gentile—you crazy damn fool—why didn't you wait? Why didn't you wait until you could be sure? For you missed him, and now we got to dig him out!"

15

IN THE DARK of the alley, Grady Haskell waited with drawn gun. On his right hand was the wall of the Canyon House, on his left that of the store, and so long as no one came up the alley behind him, here he was safe. There was, though, he realized bleakly, no uncertainty of what lay ahead. That missed shot and the savage yell which followed made everything clear enough. Rutt Dubison and his Beaverhead crowd were in Reservation, and their purpose was plain. They were here to even up, to get him, Grady Haskell!

Cold realization of this fact and its danger, did things to him. It fanned to a glow the same bitter fire that had raged in him the night he blasted Rudy Shedd to death and clubbed Rutt Dubison down in crimson unconsciousness. And it brought out the same remorseless purpose that had consumed him when he physically whipped Vince Tendler to abject surrender.

He held position, still, watchful, and saw movement along the street, furtive and cautious. Shadows that were armed men, slinking, shifting, making the most of every dark pocket as they worked a way toward him.

Off to the left there was a stir and a soft call, and then Sandy Lee was into the alley beside him.

"No!" Haskell rapped. "Get out of here, Sandy. It's my chore. You stay clear!"

"Like hell!" retorted Sandy. "Kineen and Jellick are

205

buying in, too. Milo suggests we get back in the store and the four of us fort up there. Plenty of guns on Milo's store rack."

"No!" Haskell said again. "I'm the one that gang is after. It's my chore, mine! Keep out of it!"

With the words he shot twice, throwing down on a figure darting across the moonlit street. Both shots missed. But sharp on the heels of them, from the deep dark under the store overhang a rifle lashed its thinner, harder report and that running figure went down in a long fall, rolling over and over. Came again Jim Kineen's long Hibernian howl, this time in taunting triumph.

It brought gunfire from half a dozen spots, little blobs of quick expanding, quick dissolving flame, along with racketing report and the spatting and thudding of hurtling lead, searching the alley mouth and along the store front.

Jim Kineen yelled again, challenging, taunting. Haskell swore feelingly.

"A man's friends! You bless them one moment, damn them the next. Sandy, if you're bound to be in—come on! We got to pull the shooting away from the store!"

He went back along the alley at a run, Sandy pounding after him. He cut sharp across behind the store, floundered through a small litter of trash there and kept on behind darkened buildings, heading for Jim Kineen's stable. Over in the street guns beat up a steady racket.

At the stable, Sandy said, "I won't be far," and slid away into the shadows. Haskell wheeled into the dark runway and went along it, knowing exactly what he wanted and where to find it. Now that Joe Peele was caring for the stable, Haskell had taken to leaving his rifle with his saddle, which straddled a wall peg at the end of the oat bin. He located the weapon by feel, hauled it from the boot. Here in the stable it was quiet, except for a horse that stamped and snorted softly, back in the stall area.

At the mouth of the runway again, Haskell called guardedly.

"Sandy!"

From across the street by Doc Venable's office where his horse was tied, Sandy's answer came drifting.

"Over here. Gettin' my rifle. Should you need some, I got extra shells."

"Start using them," Haskell told him. "We got to take the weight off Kineen and Jellick."

So saying, he dropped to one knee and began lacing the low shadows on each side of the street. Reaction was immediate. Come a burst of startled return fire and then a man's uneasy shout.

"They're on both sides of us, Dubison! I don't like this!"

"That's Tendler!" called Sandy Lee. "The damn renegade!"

Immediately Sandy drove rifle lead in the direction of the voice.

Over in his cabin by the river, Joe Peele had been washing up the supper dishes. He wanted to get this chore out of the way before heading down to the stable for a final checkup for the night. It had been deeply satisfying for him to have Grady Haskell and Sandy Lee sit at his frugal table and eat a meal with him. Somehow it had been symbolic of a full acceptance back into the world of solid respect and worthiness. So Joe was whistling his content as he dried and shelved a final dish.

He carried the dishwater outside to dump it. And it was at this moment the rippling echo of the night's first shot came across the house tops to him. On the heels of it lifted an angry yell and then another, one of them being intelligible enough for Joe to catch a name. Gentile! Then, within short moments, more guns opened up, flailing the night sky with hard echoes.

Joe needed no more to set him off. If Frank Gentile was in town and some shooting going on, it meant but one thing. Which was that good men were lined up against the bad ones, and his place was at the side of the good ones.

A minute later he was hurrying through the night toward the stable, aiming to come around past it and hit the street at the west end. As he ran he stuffed buckshot loads into the lethal breech of his old Greener shotgun.

A little beyond the west end of town a lone Beaverhead rider guarded a group of saddle mounts. The riders of these, Rutt Dubison and several others, had drifted quietly into town on foot, the theory being that they could thus reach certain points of vantage along the street without attracting attention or stirring up suspicion. Once they reached the vantage points a few shots would be thrown at the sky, and when the sound of these drew Deputy Grady Haskell into the street to investigate, he would be cut down, on sight and without mercy. After which, this damn town of Reservation would be hazed into a proper respect for the men of Beaverhead.

Such had been the theory. But what about the fact?

The horse guard was worried. He had heard the first shot and the quick following yell of anger from the throat of Rutt Dubison, indicating a slip-up, somewhere. Now the shooting was general, all up and down the street, even from this far west end, far too much of it for the need of killing any one man. Very plainly something had gone wrong. Cursing softly, the guard reflected that something nearly always did go wrong when you set out to buck the law. He built a nervous cigarette, sucked at it hungrily.

Once settled down to it, Grady Haskell had methodically probed the hostile dark corners along the street with his Winchester. Now the hammer fell on an empty chamber. He sent out brief call again.

"Coming over, Sandy! I can use those extra shells."

He heard the whip of a couple of slugs close behind him as he made the sanctuary of the far shadows.

"Don't you try that again!" growled Sandy. "You're the high mogul they're after, and if they get you, they got everything. Let me do the street crossin'; I don't count like you do." He shoved a handful of cartridges at Haskell, adding, "That gang eased into town on foot. I'm wondering where they left their horses. I got a notion to have a look."

"Go ahead," Haskell approved, plugging fresh loads through the magazine gate of his rifle. "You find any, scatter them, plenty! But watch yourself—there may be a guard."

Sandy Lee drifted away and Haskell again surveyed the street, with its inky side shadows and the thin silver of starlight along its open center and gleaming against the higher portions of the buildings. At the moment shooting had lessened.

In the wide outer dark, Sandy Lee had dropped back to the edge of the timber, prowling the fringe of this to the stage and freight road at the west end of the flat. Here a breath of faintly stirring night wind brought a whiff of cigarette smoke to Sandy's nostrils.

Low crouched, he went upwind like some four-footed hunter of the wild. Ahead a horse stamped the earth, sneezed gustily. Then he saw them, close grouped in the pale starlight. The smell of cigarette smoke was stronger. One guard, or more? Even closer to the earth, Sandy circled with extreme care.

The uneasiness of the horse guard had increased by the minute. Also the horses were shifty, always a bad sign. Something sure had got off the center of the trail. Every instinct in him was now crawling with apprehension. He stared with straining eyes through the night toward the street where the guns had snarled and blasted so furiously at first, but which was now quieting down. Which in itself signified something. But—what?

"You—don't move! Freeze right there!"

The order came from his left with a thin, harsh emphasis, and the guard grunted as though struck by a physical impact. His mouth jarred open and the butt of his cigarette fell, striking off a faint shower of sparks on contact with the earth.

Command came again, bleak, remorseless.

"Reach—quick! And high!"

The guard obeyed with jerky haste. There was no great toughness in this fellow, being more jackal than lion.

Sandy Lee moved quickly in and when in proper reach drove a quick, chopping blow with the barrel of his rifle. It landed solidly. The guard grunted again and slumped in a heap. Sandy located the fellow's gun and took it.

Back in town the firing had fallen to complete pause, and after the past tumult the quiet was so deep that when a great horned owl hooted, well back in the timber, the sound came across the night sky, full and round and booming.

The Beaverhead horses were now very uneasy, shifting and swinging back and forth, held by the ground tie of trailing reins, but just about ready to break in spite of such. Sandy let out a couple of shrill whoops, raised the captured gun and emptied it close above the heads of the nervous animals.

They exploded in wild scatter, like a covey of flushed quail, racing away at all angles toward the black depths of the timber. Sandy threw the emptied gun as far as he could into the dark, then trotted back toward town, well satisfied with himself.

Sandy's shrill yells and the rattle of shots he'd turned loose, carried the length and breadth of town. And after these had come the pound of massed, racing hoofs, fading into the timber. And there was no mistaking the implication of these sounds. So now consternation struck along the street of Reservation.

To a man of the saddle, be he good or bad, hardly any prospect could bring greater dismay than that of being left afoot. Such a mischance was bad enough at any time. Tonight it could be catastrophic, almost suicidal.

A quick, fading rush began along the street, men dodging from shadow to shadow, intent now on just getting out of town with a whole skin. For this whole deal had gone sour. They had missed getting the man they had come to get, and the entire town, it seemed was up in arms against them, fighting them to a standstill and beyond. Their cause had grown desperate before. Now they were afoot, their horses stampeded. It was time to be gone—long gone—!

Rutt Dubison tried to hold them. But at best these riders of his were renegades, whose primary concern in life was over their own personal welfare. There were no heroes in this crowd. They might fight for a winning cause, but never for a losing one. And this one was definitely lost.

Rutt Dubison raged and cursed at them. He ran out into the street to try and rally them. He ran too far, his lank figure a distorted shape in the starlight of the street.

Simultaneously, two rifles reawakened the echoes along the street. From the west end where Grady Haskell crouched and from the deep dark under the store overhang where Jim Kineen lurked. The lank, raging figure of Rutt Dubison jerked violently and then was down, a sprawled smudge against the shadow stained earth.

Retreat quickened, men rushing for the shelter of the open beyond town. Frank Gentile, realizing full well that the foray was a failure, went with the rest, but not with their confusion. He knew how small the chance of locating a horse that had stampeded into the far night and the timber. But in Kineen's stable there were other horses and gear. With a little luck a man might slip in there and locate something to ride!

The same kind of thought came to Vince Tendler, and he too aimed for the stable.

Coming up from his cabin and thoroughly acquainted with the place now, Joe Peele entered the stable out back and moved through the stall area to the black mouth of the runway and waited there, keening the night to locate friend or enemy. Now, abruptly, a man wheeled into the runway and Joe's challenge hit at him.

"Who is it? Name yourself!"

At this moment there existed none for whom Frank Gentile knew an atom of concern. Only Gentile counted. So his answer to Joe Peele's challenge was two quick shots, stabbing through the blackness at Joe's voice. The first missed, but the second hit. Joe Peele staggered and spun and half fell against the inner wall of the runway.

The challenge Joe Peele had thrown carried across street to the ears of Grady Haskell. Alerted by it and guided by the flashes of Gentile's gun, he swung his rifle into line and let go. The bullet struck Frank Gentile squarely between the shoulders, lifting him, then dropping him, face down and lifeless.

Joe Peele slipped slowly down against that inner wall until he was sitting, the old Greener shotgun across his knees, both barrels loaded, both hammers cocked, but the gun unfired. The swift, deep agony that had struck with Gentile's bullet, was now turning to an all-over numbness.

Charging up behind Gentile, Vince Tendler caught the flare of the rifle across from the stable. Who held the weapon he did not know or care. As Gentile had, he figured any gun now was a hostile one. From a reeking belt gun he threw shot after shot.

A leg went out from under Grady Haskell, as if hit by a club. Another blow smashed into his chest, high up on the right side. These were giant forces to wrack and twist him and leave him flattened in the dust, staring up at the frightened stars, dazed and stupified with shock.

Vince Tendler dodged into the stable runway. He stumbled over the body of Frank Gentile, went to his hands and knees on the straw littered floor. In falling he dropped his gun, and fell to cursing thickly as he clawed frantically about, trying to locate it.

As if from very far away, Joe Peele heard that cursing. Everything was far away for Joe now—feeling, sound, perception. Yet, somehow, he recognized the voice.

The weight of the Greener as he strove to lift it, was tremendous. It took everything he could master to get it up and level.

"Tendler," he sighed. "You—Tendler—!"

Desperate and wild in the unseeing blackness of the runway, Vince Tendler lunged to his feet.

The Greener blared, both barrels. The recoil tore the weapon completely out of Joe Peele's grasp. When the bellowing echoes were gone, Joe listened and listened for more of Tendler's cursing. He could hear none of it. In fact, of a sudden he could hear nothing at all—nothing. . . .

Out in the night, Grady Haskell lay, wondering. Wondering at the strange paralysis which held him so close to the earth and so unable to move. Wondering if it had been a roll of thunder that had just sounded, muffled and far away as though enclosed within walls. Wondering why the light of the stars grew fainter and fainter. . . . ?

16

It was the pain which brought him partially out of the mists. It hit him in waves, convulsing, exhausting. Particularly in his chest, where a savage torment stabbed.

People were around him, people with gruff voices and with heavy hands which gripped and hurt. He tried to curse them away from him, but they paid him no attention at all.

He caught a clear utterance by one of the voices.

"I've got to get that damned slug. If I don't, he won't have a chance. I've got to go deep, so make sure he don't move!"

So the hands held him, pressing him down, and the pain in his chest climbed and climbed until he lost the world in a sea of roaring blackness.

He was a long time in that blackness, before any light came back into it. When it did, it was a queer, strange light, which was never still and somehow, never real, and peopled with all manner of phantoms and leering demons and strange devils. This, Grady Haskell decided, was hell for sure, and he far down in the depths of it.

Then even hell went away and there were no devils, no anything, and time, it seemed, ceased to exist.

Came a day, finally, when reality returned. Not a great deal of it, just a thin fragment, and for a brief moment or two he opened his eyes and recognized the ceiling of his room above him, and saw a face bending over him, a ruddy face with shrewd, kindly eyes under a towering shock of white hair. A face that smiled and spoke comforting words.

"How we hung on to you, son—I don't know. But we did, and you're back with us to stay."

After which, he slept.

Time returned, separated into its comforting, familiar components of night and day. People came back, people he knew. Mrs. Wall, bustling, kind, efficient, and Ruby Peele, very quiet, very gentle, took turns feeding him. Doc Venable, he of the ruddy face, the shrewd, wise eyes and snowy mop of hair, changed bandages on his chest and leg and, with the aid of Jim Kineen, bathed him and rolled him in clean, cool sheets. One day Kineen shaved him, growling and scolding gruffly.

" 'Tis a great nuisance you are! Getting yourself shot and afterwards throwing fever fits until you were nothing but skin and bone and scaring the seven wits out of all of us. There were times when I felt like taking a club to you, that I did!"

A slow grin touched Haskell's gaunt face, and his words fell slow and careful.

"I remember people holding me down and hurting me. You must have been one of them. I remember cussing all of you—and good!"

Kineen's answering grin was kindly.

"That you did, and scandalously. But it was at a time when violent language might be expected. For with Sandy Lee and Amos Potter and me holding you down, Doc Venable finally managed to dig a forty-five slug out of your chest. If he hadn't got it, my friend, you wouldn't be here, now."

"The showdown on the street," said Haskell, his face going sober again. "I want the story on that. How did it all come out?"

"Like this," Kineen said, putting his razor away. "They lost Rutt Dubison, Frank Gentile, Vince Tendler and two others."

"They did plenty of shooting," reminded Haskell. "They must have hit somebody besides me."

"One man," Jim Kineen said gravely. "A very good man."

"Who?"

"I am without help again in the stable."

"Joe!" exclaimed Haskell. "Joe Peele! Dead—?"

Kineen's head went slowly up and down. "But before he went he got the one who near did for you. Vince Tendler."

Haskell rolled his head on the pillow, looked out the sunlit window.

"Joe," he murmured. "Joe Peele. And just when his world had turned good again. How do you know he got Tendler, and that it was Tendler who downed me?"

Kineen explained. Three dead men were found in the stable runway. Each had died by a different gun. Buckshot from Joe Peele's Greener had done for Vince Tendler. A .41 Colt had killed Joe Peele, and Frank Gentile had carried a .41 Colt. Gentile himself had died from a rifle bullet.

"That could have been my shot," Haskell said. "I threw one that way."

"We figured so," Kineen admitted. "You were the only one in a position to have reached Gentile at that time. According to the shells still in his belt, Tendler was packing a .45 and there was a .45 Colt lying near him, all chambers fired. And," finished Kineen with some emphasis, "the two slugs Doc Venable dug out of you were .45s. So there you have it."

Haskell rolled his head again. "Why did it have to be Joe—?"

That evening it was Ruby Peele who brought his supper.

"I just heard about your father," Haskell said gravely. "He was a good man, Ruby—a damn good man!"

He saw the quick tears start and she turned away for a moment, nodding.

"A good man," repeated Haskell. "There was one thing he wanted above everything—that he make you truly proud of him. You can be proud of him, Ruby. All your life you can be proud."

Presently she turned back, her eyes still moist, but otherwise composed. Her voice was steady. She had courage, Ruby Peele did.

"All my life I will be proud," she said simply. "And Neal, my Neal—he's proud, too."

"Your Neal," proclaimed Haskell, "is a very lucky boy."

She stood gazing down at him, hardly out of girlhood, hardly into womanhood, yet a bit of both. Quickly she bent, brushing her lips against his cheek.

"Thank you for everything, Grady Haskell."

Then she was quickly gone.

Next day came a real surprise. Haskell heard the stage creak into town and shortly after it was Bill Hoe who walked into the room.

"Well, well," he observed cheerfully, "you had to go and stop a slug, did you?"

"Two of them," corrected Haskell, grinning. "Bill, I'm sure glad to see you. There's a lot to explain. I couldn't get it all in that letter."

"You got enough," declared the sheriff as he gripped Haskell's hand. "You've done a fine job, son. Your suggestion I check on Breedon's past was a good one. I didn't like what I found, but I found it. Breedon had once done time for cattle rustling. He sure fooled me. When I hired him on as a deputy, I figured him clean. He wasn't."

"And when he got up here in the Trinities and saw what a fat target Hayfork could be, he decided to throw in with Dubison's crowd and try for free beef again," summarized Haskell.

"That's about it," Bill Hoe agreed. "I been working the law pretty much all my life and I've found that men don't change very often. Most generally, once a renegade, always a renegade. And the lure of free beef. The life-long dream of the confirmed rustler. Once they get a taste of it, they never get over it, seems like. Same as with a sheep-killing dog. About the way of Breedon's death, son—you figure you got the real truth on that?"

"Sure of it, Bill. Dead sure!"

"Why then, that's good enough for me. When this fellow Jim Levening you wrote me about, gets able to give it, we'll get a deposition of fact from him for the record, and close the case. They tell me you already took care of Gentile, personally. Which just about cleans this particular slate. All you got to do now is loaf and get well."

"The toughest chore of all," Haskell vowed. "What are you going to do?"

Bill Hoe chuckled. "What the boys up around the State Capitol would call repairing my political fences. Seeing as I'm here, I might as well get out and meet the folks."

Piled up warmth put Haskell to sleep again. When he woke, the shadows of late afternoon were stealing down from the timber, and he had the feeling that someone was watching him. He turned his head and saw her, standing in the doorway, and a great gladness rushed through him.

"Katie! Katie Levening!"

Slowly she moved into the room.

"So often I've wondered how it would be when I saw you again," he said eagerly. "And each time you are more lovely than the last. Why is that, Kattie Levening? Do you mind me asking?"

Her eyes were very soft. "No," she said gently. "I don't mind."

She came up to his bedside, looking down at him. "I have talked with Sheriff Hoe. He was very kind. I need have no more fears. And no one can guess how great the relief. First Dad to worry over. Then—then you."

"Me! You worried over me? That was kindness, Katie Levening."

"Kindness? Agony you mean—dreadful, complete agony. When—when Sandy brought word that you were wounded, maybe dying—oh, Grady, Grady— you can't imagine—"

She dropped down on the edge of the bed, eyes flooding, tears glistening on her cheeks.

"Why, Katie," he murmured, wondering. "All this—for me?"

She nodded very fast, as a little girl might, and then she was framing his gaunt face with her hands and her lips were a warmth and a fragrance on his.

Afterwards, when she drew away, her laugh was soft and rich and somewhat shaky.

"If that were shameless, I don't care. For now we are even!"

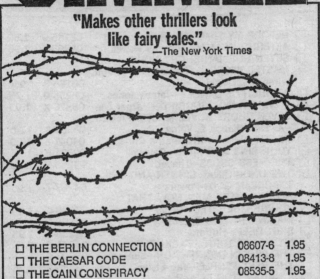

ALL TIME BESTSELLERS FROM POPULAR LIBRARY

FREE
Fawcett Books Listing

There is Romance, Mystery, Suspense, and Adventure waiting for you inside the Fawcett Books Order Form. And it's yours to browse through and use to get all the books you've been wanting . . . but possibly couldn't find in your bookstore.

This easy-to-use order form is divided into categories and contains over 1500 titles by your favorite authors.

So don't delay—take advantage of this special opportunity to increase your reading pleasure.

Just send us your name and address and 35¢ (to help defray postage and handling costs).

FAWCETT BOOKS GROUP
P.O. Box C730, 524 Myrtle Ave., Pratt Station, Brooklyn, N.Y. 11205

Name_____
            (please print)

Address_____
City_____ State_____ Zip_____
Do you know someone who enjoys books? Just give us their names and addresses and we'll send them an order form too!

Name_____
Address_____
City_____ State_____ Zip_____

Name_____
Address_____
City_____ State_____ Zip_____